Quantum Voices

A Novel

Stephen Spotte

OPEN BOOKS

Published by Open Books

To John Hanchette, *in memoriam*

Pulitzer Prize-winning investigative journalist, reprobate and
raconteur, exemplary drinking companion

Numquam minus solus quam cum solus.
Marcus Tullius Cicero, *De Officiis*

AND SO WE WERE AT WAR. Dawn. The opaque gray light. The shifting stink of shitfields. The stink of ourselves. Translucent mist condensing on his neck, sliding sinuously underneath the eighty-pound pack that stuck to his shirt that stuck to the skin of his back already slimy and foul at that early hour like the epidermis of an amphibian.

It appeared, as always, with the fevered sun, teasing, gripping his ankles from behind and threatening to trip him with every step until he wanted to scream to be left alone. Near noon, as the sun approached its zenith, it crept beneath the soles of his boots, popping out like sheaves of black flypaper whenever he lifted a heel. There was nothing to be done. In the afternoon, the pattern reversed: then it pulled him forward, gripping his ankles from the front and causing him to stumble and glance down warily through sweat-smeared eyes. Gravity affects time and imprisons us. Live upstairs and your life will move ahead faster than if you lived on the lower floor. Similarly, time runs slower at our feet than at our heads. You can imagine it, omitting the dilatory nature of friction, each footstep harder to take than the last while your head presses forward with less effort, bobbing along for the ride.

The usual drill went like this. A briefing in the afternoon before insert: number of days in the field, call signs, prospective drinking water situation, who walked point and tail-end Charlie. With a full fireteam of nine it was easy divvying up the order, but now they were five. That night packing for noise reduction by stuffing cans of C-rats inside socks and taping dog tags together, deciding how many canteens to tote and how much ammo, all the while conscious of weight. The pack held the resources to keep you alive, but it was also your enemy, intent on exhausting you. Then a few hours of sleepless unease, on the move at dawn waiting for the chopper, clambering aboard, a short flight to a landing zone in a "hot" place of known danger called Indian Country, sometimes prolonged by zigs and zags and even a fake landing to fool Charlie about the real destination. Jumping out at the LZ and running for the wood line or dropping into elephant grass and crawling. Brief pause after dismount for a head count, then days of humping, nights of setting perimeter and trying to sleep while wondering if the enemy would slip through the defenses and cut your throat. We communicate in military jargon, a sort of pidgin. We use it for two reasons. It abbreviates and thus streamlines language, making it more efficient just as mathematics is reduced to symbols; and it enhances the sense of camaraderie. We are "brothers" because we speak a common language not spoken or generally understood by civilians.

◊ ◊ ◊

They were headed east on a roadbed of powdered red clay the consistency of talc. There had not been a breeze in days. This was the dry season, the sky empty of rain. During monsoon they had trudged miserably along similar roads through ankle-deep red mud, cursing the importunate wetness and wondering if the sun would ever return. They had been thrown together involuntarily and become inseparable, each other's uneasy assurance and constant annoyance.

The traffic had attenuated to a trickle of M-113 APCs transporting Marines east augmented by supply convoys and the rare angel track hurrying toward the front. At the moment they faced nothing more pressing than servitude and the physical discomforts of being overdressed grunts in a tropical climate. Chronic inflammation of crotch and ass stung with each step, feet slid damply inside boots raising blisters that never healed. Then there was athlete's foot, the soft skin peeling off the bottoms of his feet, the itching between the toes. In childhood they went barefoot starting in May, feet calloused as shoe leather, except during the coldest months. He wondered whether Marines should shuck boots and socks. In bare feet they could feel the contours of the ground, conform with its protean shapes and textures. Now, between feet and the earth were layers of unfeeling substance. Anax soaked his socks in Halazone-water and stored them damp in plastic bags. He said it kills the fungus that causes athlete's foot.

They wore bandanas over their faces to keep from inhaling the dust, which quickly became slime against lips and noses. He thought of Pa emerging black-faced from the mine, eyes ringed in white but the rest of him blackened with coal dust, black as night, black as vantablack. Black like Pa's hidden-away lungs. He trudged on. Of himself, only his shadow was black.

For the present they were safe from attack and sniper fire and incoming artillery, this area of III Corps being under control of the U.S. military backed by ARVN, although they were about to cross into a region of active combat. Second lieutenant Murphy was still hopeful of an insert into the tactical zone, but the requested choppers had been delayed, then deployed elsewhere. Orders had come to keep humping. The men were now strung along the road, bitching and trudging toward the objective.

He pictured the LT: medium-built leaning toward thin, sandy hair, unable to hide his unease. And a peculiar mannerism. When addressing them he was always rubbing the backs of the fingers of his right hand against his pantleg, as if polishing the Academy ring he wore on the ringer finger. Or maybe the ring stood as a constant reminder of who he was supposed to be, of a man impersonating himself.

The platoon had been undermanned by more than a squad during three weeks in the safe zone. The LT had been promised reinforcements, but time was running short. Meanwhile, he was doubling as leader of one remaining squad and leaving platoon sergeant Barnes in command of the other. Barnes had just four men plus himself, not enough to fill two standard fireteams of four each, so he combined them under team leader corporal Anax Grayson. They had no corpsman.

◊ ◊ ◊

His sense of self could fracture spontaneously anywhere at any instant, although certain situations and states—exhaustion, extreme physical or mental discomfort—could release the effect. Monotony might cause the brain's left hemisphere to lose dominance, dimming his perception of reality and introducing a strange sense of hyperawareness. Another possibility: a subject so affected is forced to exist in an extremely focused state of the moment in which time slips past unnoticed. When it happened the sensation of disembodiment flooded his being followed by the hallucination of a strange yet familiar presence, someone he had known all his life. He might recognize the specter as his disembodied self; alternatively, as a clone of himself but a distinctly separate individual—his *doppelgänger*. At such moments, the specialized patches of neurons within his infero-temporal cortex remained quiescent, not firing and failing to execute the response necessary to recognize a face.

The heat, the biting insects, the exhaustion combined to trigger the effect this time. He glimpsed his tormenter beside him on the left, aping his slouch and shuffling gait, the swing of his arms, the forward tilt of his head as if under the same stress and the weight of an equal burden. They glanced sideways at each other. Jeeter, his double to the left, was grinning. It was Jeeter shapeshifting into his shadow who had tugged him back at mid-morning, peeked from underneath his heels at noon, and at this moment was dragging him reluctantly forward through the waning afternoon.

Jaws clenched, he tried unsuccessfully to swallow the outburst. "Stop hit!"

He and Anax were walking side by side, Anax six feet on his right. "What?" Anax said, mildly startled.

"Nothin. Sorry." And under his breath, "I warn't talkin to you."

"Who, then? There's no one else nearby."

"Myself, I reckon. . .sort of." He pointedly gazed around, a ruse to make Anax think he was absorbing the scenery, as might a connoisseur of landscapes. Jeeter had vanished, melting again into shadow. He looked down and saw the distorted silhouette stretched in front, liquid and black, slithering and rippling over the hot stones, tilting as he tilted, leaning as he leaned. It could be no one else. He was aware of the combined mass of his body and pack; he heard the scrunch of his own footfalls, felt the force reverberate upward into his spine, and wondered if humanity had always walked on its hindlegs.

◊ ◊ ◊

The day was past noon when Staff Sergeant Barnes called a break. They sprawled heat-dazed and surated in the shade of a large tree, leaves dulled russet by road dust, sipping canteen water and fumbling in packs for C-rats. No one was hungry, but training had inculcated the need of food for endurance. The road had defiladed them, but they would soon move overland toward the tactical zone and on approaching it join Lieutenant Murphy's squad. For the present there was no need of safety in numbers. The rumbling vehicles had become intermittent, opening acoustic space for bird calls and the stridulations of insects, and allowing the air to clear a little.

Barnes unfolded a sweat-stained map and made a notation of their location. "RTO Weasel," he said in a falsetto voice, "jump on that there ray. . .dee. . .oh and call us in."

Weasel cranked the Prick-25, raising static and eventually a response. "Surprised this fucker works. I was sure we'd be out of range, and we left the big antenna back at base."

Barnes took the mike and identified himself. He gave their position and direction of future movement and asked might they be in line for an airlift anytime soon. "Negative," said the disembodied voice. "Orders are to keep humping. Same thing I just told your LT. We got eyes in the sky on y'all. Another few clicks or so northeast and you'll bump into one another."

"If y'all's already in the air then why ain't y'all stoppin by to give us a ride?" said Barnes.

"Over," said the voice. The connection went dead.

Barnes looked up. "Shit, you heard the man. No rest for God's chilluns." Some of the men had pulled off boots and socks. Barnes did likewise and examined his mangled feet. Weasel stopped in the act of lighting a cigarette. "Jesus, Barnesie, you ain't got any toes. Holy shit, what happened?"

Barnes sighed. "Chosin Reservoir happened. You know that, so dont be a smartass." He dug into his boots and extracted a soggy sock from each, folded them together, and put them in his rucksack. He took out and separated a fresh pair and stuffed one sock into the toe of each boot.

The others gathered to gawk. He looked hard at

them and watched their gazes transfer uneasily to the distance, their subtle shifting revealing uncertainty of place. "Ain't none of you dumb bastards seed feet before? If'n you had the sense to look down you'd find two of your own."

"Yeah, but I got all ten toes on mine," said Donut. There was hesitant chuckling. No one in the squad was older than twenty except Anax and Barnes, a hardened Korean vet of thirty-four. He was usually genial, although still intimidating. Here was someone who had really been in the shit.

◊ ◊ ◊

"Okay, so listen up. I ain't a-goin to tell this story more'n once." He explained how he had been in Korea at Chosin Reservoir with Fox company in the winter of 1950, his squad assigned to defend a hilltop overlooking the road from the south, the only source of supplies and reinforcements. It was twenty-five below zero with a ripping wind, the ground so hard they could only chip at it with entrenching tools. It was like digging in concrete. They had been on the march for hours and when arriving at what would become basecamp it was nearly dark. The men were cold, hungry, and exhausted. They bitched and wondered why the officers seemed so keen on setting a perimeter when instead they could grab some hot chow, sack out, and dig foxholes in the morning. As it turned out, the officers knew best.

The perimeter was horseshoe shaped. The Red Chinese attacked that night and every night for two weeks, and they made no secret about it. They blew bugles and clanged cymbals and charged the hill in waves. One night out there in the wind and blackness some invisible asshole even played taps. When they poured over the ridge the dug-in Marines hunkered down and cut loose. There were so many and they were so close that aiming was superfluous. They fired the M1s on automatic and mowed down the enemy like advancing fields of cornstalks. The Chinese resembled chunky rabbits in their white uniforms, or snowmen suddenly grown legs. He paused then and said quietly, almost to himself, that gooks are not all the same and how strange it is that the Vietnamese wear white in mourning and black in war.

Even in the face of blistering fire they kept coming, and eventually the Marines were overrun. Then it was hand-to-hand. Guys out of ammo grabbed the entrenching tools they had been cussing and swung them like baseball bats. Marines always collect their dead, but not the Chinese. They dragged back only the frozen bodies conveniently nearby where they stacked them unceremoniously like sandbags for field fortifications. The Marines did the same with the dead Chinese, arranging them to fortify the rims of their foxholes.

"Anyhow," said Barnes, "after four nights and three days on that mountain we got a reprieve. I couldn't feel my feet nor stand proper, so I shucked the boots and had a look-see. When I pulled off the socks they rattled like they was filled with marbles. When I peeked inside 'em I seed my toes, black and froze solid."

"Why didn't you get out of the Corps with a disability when you rotated back to the World?" said Ray-Ban.

Barnes looked at him contemptuously. "And do what? Go back to Kentucky and fish? Raise hogs? Shoot squirrels? Marry a mountain cutie missin most of her teeth like me and spawn a bunch of splay-foot kids with runny noses? Naw, I'm Mother Green all the way. But I had to fight with the higher-highers to stay active duty. The bastards profiled me and said that without toes I was unfit for infantry. Horseshit, I told 'em. Hell, my trigger finger come through the Chosin jist fine. I dint pull the trigger with my toes. Take me out to the obstacle course and I'll prove hit, I told 'em. And I could've. I'd been practicin. With socks jammed in the toes of my boots I run the course good as any grunt. That plus my combat experience got me back. *Oorah!*"

"With all them years in uniform, then why are you still a E-6?" Weasel again. Barnes gave a toothless grin.

"When I got reinstated after Korea they promoted me to E-7. But I like to drink, and when I drink I like to fight, and when I fight git busted down and have to claw back up the ranks. You know. . . ." He made a motion like an ocean wave, up and down.

◊ ◊ ◊

When the Korean conflict ended with no clear winner he and hundreds of other Marines returned to Camp Lejeune for mustering out. Several weeks passed. He was not ready to be a civilian and eventually found himself standing at attention before a standard-issue metal desk waiting to be acknowledged. The major sitting at the desk was studying an open file, slowly flipping the pages using fingers resembling misaligned pieces of a puzzle. When at last he looked up Barnes snapped to attention and saluted.

"At ease," said the major. "Sergeant Barnes?"

"Yessir."

"I've just been reading your file. Impressive, some of it. Silver Star from the Chosin, several disciplinary actions before and after Korea. Overall, the career of a solid Marine, even a hero. Why are you contesting an honorable discharge with lifetime disability benefits? Seems like a good deal."

"Not to me, sir. I'm a lifer or want to be. I was orphaned and fostered out, last time to a farm. When I turned fourteen and did a man's work for what should've been a day's pay they told me I was lucky to git room and board, then bitched that I ate too much. Many's the night I bedded down in the hay-loft wrapped in a horse blanket 'cause the heat risin from the livestock made hit warmer than sleepin in the goddamn basement. So I enlisted soon's I could. That old farmer signed me up and was glad to see me go. Said I warn't worth the money the state give him. Mother Green's the only mother ever give a shit about me. She's give me ever'thin I needed 'cept a tit to suck. I git solid food, clean clothes, a reg'lar bed, and comrades who have my back. The Marines is all I know, and I dont ask nothin 'cept to stay a field Marine."

The major's face was crisscrossed by scars, his smile like a ruptured blister. "I understand."

"I see you got the SSM too, sir. Where was hit you was in the soup?"

"Iwo Jima. Messed up my face, hands, and arms, but

I can still jockey a desk. You expect to be a field Marine without toes? Doesn't it fuck with your balance?"

"At first, but I figgered that out. You see, I shove a heavy sock into the end of each boot to take up the space of toes, then walk flat-footed so's I dont tip forward. And I wear my boots only a coupla months. That holds ever'thin together inside, long as they stay tight. When they go soft and loose I requisition another pair. Hell, sir, I could run a obstacle course good as them cherries jist out of basic and then do a day's hump with my rifle and pack. I kin prove hit if you want. Jist send me back to active duty."

The major shook his head. "Not necessary to prove anything. I believe you. We need experienced Marines. With Southeast Asia heating up we'll be in the soup again sooner than later. I'm approving your request to remain active duty and recommending bumping you up a rank. Stay out of trouble."

"I'll try, and thank you sir." He saluted and turned to leave.

"One more thing, sergeant."

"Yessir?"

"Did your platoon have an E-1 named Hatfield?"

"We did, sir. On'ry cuss, lotta small disciplinary checks on his record." He stood at attention, waiting.

"I ask because I remembered seeing the paperwork on him. Lay down in his foxhole when the shit was flying, leaving his mate to take on the Chinese by himself. Do you remember that?"

"I recall hearin about hit sir, but I was in another foxhole and dint see hit myself. I never met the man. He was in a diff'rent squad, but I heered he was from

Logan County, West Virginia. I'm from Pike County, Kentucky, practically next door."

"Well, you might like to know he received an Other than Honorable discharge. Better than a Duck Dinner. But that OTH on his DD-214 is there for life. It means he's not entitled to any benefits, and the yellow bastard sure as hell doesn't deserve any. Cowardice in the Corps is rare, but pops up occasionally." The major returned to his paperwork. "Good luck, sergeant," he said without looking up.

◊ ◊ ◊

Journal entry My name is Anaximander Dyson Grayson. I am presently a corporal in the U.S. Marine Corps stationed in Vietnam in the midst of a war. My job is reconnaissance, helping to collect information during field patrols that might be of use to those planning military actions in the regions where my team is deployed. I am by education and training a neuroscientist. I joined the military for a chance to study American combatants in the field with the expectation of later writing a book on the manifestations of stress and their neurological origins under life-threatening circumstances. Stated differently, I sought to actualize my research with personal experience by direct participation with my subjects instead of studying them *post hoc* in a clinical setting. Both methods have bias issues, but my choice is the more unusual and better suited to assessment through narrative instead of quantification.

Our time in uniform is likely to be the defining period in our lives. No subsequent events as civilians will likely match its intensity and range of emotions. Nothing that happens subsequently will make us feel as alive, so aware of "living in the moment." It is this psychological arena, this living laboratory, that I hope to explore from the inside using myself and fellow grunts as subjects. The effort will not be conventional science with experimental controls and statistical analyses of the results, but rather a personal probe of the enlisted man's psyche under duress: not combat alone, but the persistence of daily discomforts such as heat, rain, insects, minor though chronic maladies and diseases, homesickness, and nearly inedible food. For this reason I declined both medical and line officer commissions and enlisted as a regular recruit.

War is distinguished from other endeavors by its immediacy and the mechanisms by which it recalibrates the mind's awareness of time. This and tangential effects on the brain's neural wiring, the very reality of time and space as perceived by macro-organisms like ourselves, the subtleties of proprioception under duress, and the sense of self and agency, are inevitably reshaped by experiences of war and impinge on episodic memory, the capacity to associate memories of events with specific times and place and opening avenues for future predictions based on this archived history. In the coming months they also will test my own semantic memory involving all I know from studying the human brain and its workings.

I was born and grew up an only child in New Jersey where my father was a physics professor at Princeton University, my mother a homemaker. Dad considered himself ordinary, and I suppose he was, in context. He was bright but not brilliant, his star scarcely rivaling the shine of the great physicists and mathematicians with whom he interacted, if superficially. He was a man of comfortable self-assurance, contented within himself. He enjoyed helping the graduate students brew coffee and set out pastries for seminars when some Olympian figure came to lecture, saw no injustice in having been assigned to teach introductory classes, and was thrilled merely to trail behind listening as luminaries such as Einstein and Dirac strolled the shaded sidewalks quietly debating the intricacies of the quantum world, oblivious to his presence. Early hominins sometimes left footprints along muddy shores since turned to stone. Einstein and Dirac left no such traces. In their wake were theories and equations as proof they were here. Will this distinction matter when the world ends in fire?

Unlike most of his department colleagues, Dad actually liked sitting in a back-row seat, graciously relinquishing his rightful place near the front to a student while giants of his profession scribbled obstruse equations on chalkboards. You could say I was programmed to be a physicist, the subject having dominated my early life, but when the day came to choose a path I put aside secrets of the cosmos in favor of equally ineffable mysteries of the human brain. Nonetheless, those years of inculcation never dimmed an early love of physics, and quantum physics especially.

My name has always seemed a curiosity to others, so I shall explain it to close this posting. I was named after Anaximander, a Greek philosopher who lived 2,600 years ago and is considered by many the founder of modern science. One of Anaximander's achievements was to release Earth from its plinth and allow it to float. In his philosophy Earth is circular, not a globe but a squat cylinder having a height one-third the diameter of its base. Anaximander also deduced that "up" and "down" are the same everywhere on Earth's surface, that people standing on the opposite side of the world look up at the sky and down at their feet, just as the Greeks do. My middle name is in honor of Paul Dirac, the great English mathematician, and an early founder of quantum physics. I vaguely remember Dirac as a shy, quietly distracted man. His strange Bristol accent, the English equivalent of an American regional dialect, stayed with him for life. In contrast, his schoolmate Archie Leach, who emigrated to America and became the film star Cary Grant, washed himself of Bristol's vestiges and learned to speak like an upper-crust Bostonian.

If I am killed I hope this journal survives and falls into sympathetic hands, someone who might see its value and send it eventually to the library at Princeton. That will be you, future reader. If you are reading this posting then I am dead. The library's mailing address and phone number are provided on the end page. The librarians have on file a letter from me alerting them to perhaps expect it someday, presuming it survives me. Feel free to photocopy the contents before sending it off and apply any useful information in your own work. My only interest in seeing the journal preserved is toward advancing knowledge of the human mind. So much for my history. I am not special.

◊ ◊ ◊

Journal entry Future reader, a comment on two on the journal's peculiarities. You will notice that postings have no times and dates, a bias indoctrinated by physicists. The equations of physics do not distinguish between past and future; time does not "flow" or even exist in much of theory. Newton was incorrect in believing that it exists as an autonomous entity, uniform and unchangeable, and that "true," or "mathematical," time is imperceptible and knowable only by calculation. The modern incarnation of Newtonian time is the gravitational field, also called *spacetime*, and exists independently even in the absence of matter, as Newton thought. About this he was correct. Newtonian space, however, became Einstein's gravitational field, his theory of general relativity. Einstein showed that Newton's apple fell not from gravitational pull but as a result of Earth's curvature of spacetime in the region of the apple. Knowing such things I see no reason for granting to time a lofty perch it does not deserve, and for my purposes the concept is largely superfluous. Entries, therefore, are temporally nonspecific except in a circadian context (e.g. night, day, morning, afternoon). Dates on a calendar are arbitrary and irrelevant too, and I decline to post them.

Earth rotates fifteen degrees each hour. There are twenty-four time zones, each fifteen degrees of longitude wide. The moon rotates once in making a complete orbit of Earth. Thus, the same side always faces us, and we never see the moon's dark side. Someday soon humankind will step onto the moon and perhaps even inhabit it. For those standing on its surface, Earth's time zones will be meaningless. Should the moon be assigned its own arbitrary time zones? A possibility, although following this illustrious moment we might reprise the nature of time altogether and go in a different direction, perhaps taking as a model Borges' imaginary planet Tlön where tigers are transparent and the towers are made of blood. On Tlön, classifying a state of mind is sufficient to falsify it. There, the present is without definition, the future comprises only hope, and the past begins and ends with memory of the moment.

A leaf flutters past, dislodged from a branch. The nearer it comes to my mass the more time slows for it. I must tell my fellow grunts that the passing of time is illusory. Ignore it, I shall say. Time is beyond your control except in special situations, as when Odysseus and Penelope, reunited after twenty years, urged Athena to slow time so they could extend the intimacy of their reunion. Or if, like Joshua, you have the ear of God. It was Joshua in the Hebrew Bible who petitioned God to stop the sun's movement giving the Israelites the extended daylight needed to win a crucial battle. But for us grunts time spent at base is meaningless, irrelevant. Time in the field, ditto. Pay no attention to time; it does not exist as the entity you think it is. So. . .one foot in front of the other. Repeat.

◊ ◊ ◊

Journal entry We march along in mutual degrees of discomfort, complaining as soldiers have done since the advent of war. Future reader, assume my words have been conceived and recorded under duress. I can add little to what others have said on the subject and doubtless will continue to describe when this conflict ends. I write in pencil as I was taught in first-year chemistry. Spills are common in laboratories, and ink runs and smears; pencil marks do not. In these same classes I was taught that when making an error or wishing to change an entry, draw a line through the original instead of erasing it. In doing so you leave a trail illuminating the history of your work that others can follow. The pencils issued to us had no erasers. Here in Vietnam erasers would quickly become useless from rain and sweat.

◊ ◊ ◊

They went rabbit hunting early one fall day when Pa was working swing shift and had the morning off. Just the two of them. Such moments together were rare, and he was excited. They carried the four-ten, plenty of kick for a ten-year-old. It was October, and the mountains flashed red and yellow. They emerged from the dappled light of the woods into an abandoned cornfield that looked to have been fallow for several years and was overgrown with goldenrod and joe-pye weed higher than his head. Their disturbance flushed several rabbits, one of which stopped not a dozen feet in front of them. Jeeter was carrying the shotgun. He raised it, pulled back the hammer, and fired, feeling the kickback against his shoulder. The rabbit emitted several rapid shrieks sounding almost like a baby in agony. Its legs twitched, then it lay where it fell breathing heavily. He and Pa bent over it, watching it kick feebly and die, its eyes staring directly at him. He let go of the shotgun and dropped to the ground blubbering, face a comingling of tears and snot, knowing the danger but helpless to avoid it. "I'm sorry. I'm so sorry I shot you." He reached out and touched the rabbit, feeling its furry warmth. The next thing he felt was the inevitable fist to the side of his head. He saw stars and heard Pa shout, "You goddamn coward! You make me ashamed!"

◊ ◊ ◊

Journal entry we radioed our position to base and received the expected but still unnerving response: we have entered Indian Country. Each wonders silently about the quickness of his reaction in case of an ambush. Human perception can resolve time to about a tenth of a second. During this interval light travels some thirty thousand kilometers.

We close ranks, shift the collective consciousness to high alert, and hope for the best. Sharpening attentional agency narrows focus to certain features in the landscape, highlighting and separating them from the background. By identifying combinations of characteristics a phenomenal scene can be isolated, reducing ambiguity. The process is enhanced by our training and experience. The effect overall is to heighten consciousness. Unfortunately, consciousness has shortcomings, the most dangerous of which is the delusion of being conscious.

The fields of elephant grass are no less tall and thick than those we passed previously along the road, but they seem more menacing, the edges of the leaves more cutting and abrasive. The stalks, set thickly, look impenetrable. What does their denseness conceal? From now on securing the perimeter at night will be a serious concern. No smoking after dark to alert Charlie of our position. No conversations above a whisper, and then only when necessary. Step quietly—and carefully; IEDs could be anywhere, cleverly made and artfully camouflaged devices sometimes fashioned from C-rat containers and other items of our own trash left behind. Avoid walking on obvious paths, Charlie's favorite places for stringing tripwires to buried explosives. Take up assigned single-file positions. Barnesie has volunteered to walk point with Donut behind him stepping in his steps, followed by Weasel carrying the Prick-25, then Anax. Skeeter draws tail-end Charlie to cover our backs. He turns frequently, head swiveling. The real Charlie, a euphemism for the Viet Cong, is sneaky, indigenous to the land. He tiptoes on little cat feet and could be somewhere behind us. Donut, intense curator of his personal terrors, whispers a life-long fear of tigers; Barnesie whispers in reply to shut the fuck up, that tigers only live in zoos because the gooks have skinned and eaten the rest.

◊ ◊ ◊

Journal entry I have found in Skeeter Hatfield, a fellow member of our five-man fireteam, an ideal recipient of my scholarly rants. Skeeter was raised in a coal camp in southern West Virginia called Scalded Creek. He is my friend, and I do not intend this to be disrespectful, but I find in him a perfect manifestation of a *tabula rasa*, the empty drawer. He understands nothing of what I babble about, but babble I must. I require more than my projected voice; the message must be received as properly formulated language by a recipient. That it will not be comprehended is a given, and also irrelevant for my needs. The tree falling in a deserted forest is not the conundrum most suppose; it represents the distinction between hearing and physics.

The first requires a listener, a recipient of the sound; the second, being simply a pressure wave, does not. Furthermore, the exercise of speaking instead of merely thinking necessitates organization of content, forcing me to be both tutor and student, adding a measure of objectivity as if imparted by an invisible coauthor. The sound of my words impinging on other ears is not much different than if the sound originated with someone else. If they seem false to my own ears then I shall consider them such. My mind needs the distillation of information for clarity as desperately as my cells require oxygen. I must speak my thoughts and continue to scribble them in this journal. For these purposes Skeeter's simultaneous presence and absence are perfect.

◊ ◊ ◊

Journal entry Skeeter had an "episode" of some sort several days ago. We were still strung along the road headed, it seemed, nowhere. Nothing except heat haze and dust ahead. He and I were walking side by side with the usual six feet separating us, when he suddenly pivoted left and struck out at the air with his closed right fist. Then he yelled, "Lemme me alone, you bastard, I'd like to kill you!" Instinctively, I looked his way and saw no one else near him. He punched the air again. I hesitate to label this as a conventional seizure because although a change in behavior was evident his muscles did not suddenly freeze, nor did he twitch or become unable to speak. Instead, the sequence ended when he tripped and fell face-forward in the dust. I dropped my pack, hurried to him, and turned him over to check if he swallowed his tongue. He had not, but his eyes were rolled up into his head, and he was babbling nonsense and vigorously trying to push me away like I was an attacking enemy. When I looked up Sergeant Barnes, having heard the commotion, was leaning over us, and the rest of the team was gathering around.

The sergeant said, "What's the matter with him, corporal? Kin you give him somethin?"

I replied that I was neither a corpsman nor a physician. Barnes said, "The LT told me you was a doctor."

I said, "I am, but I have a Ph.D., not a medical degree."

"You're the onliest thing to a corpsman we got, so you decide what we do."

"Give him some water. Then let's get him on his feet and put him in the shade for a little while, sort of monitor him."

Barnesie stood and looked at me. "Should we radio base and call in a medivac?"

"I don't think that's necessary, but I'm not an expert at trauma medicine. He seems to be recovering.

Someone pick up his pack." Barnes shouldered it and reached for the rifle without waiting for a volunteer. I said, "Donut, help me lug him to that tree across the road."

Skeeter recovered quickly, and within a half-hour we were once again on the hump, him walking beside me. I asked what had happened.

"Same shit, but usually I dont fall down. That's the heat and the weight workin agin me."

"What does 'same shit' mean?"

"Means I seed his tormentin self, like I allus do, standin right thar, angry in the face and threatenin to kill me." He nodded to the left, indicating the position of this invisible being. "He's right beside of me now, laughin. I need to kill the motherfucker a-fore he kills me, but all my life I ain't been able to grab a-holt of him. If I dont he ain't never gonna let me be." With this he clammed up, except to add, "Leastways I reckon hit's him, 'cept when I git confused and think hit's me. Then I ponder on stickin the barrel of this hyur rifle in my mouth and pullin the trigger, as he's allus tellin me to."

◊ ◊ ◊

"Okay, Skeeter, ready for my first lecture? I promise to keep it short." The sun was just peering over the horizon, but already they were on the hump, sweating and shaking out the kinks accumulated from a night of bivouacking.

"I reckon."

"Right. Here goes. Heat is unable to pass from

something cold to something hot, and this single essential law of physics separates past from future. There aren't any others. So, reduce the workings of the universe to mathematics and time's arrow is manifested only in the presence of heat. Like now." Anax laughed, offering a light mood.

"Plenty of that hyur." Skeeter grunted.

"Entropy increases with time, and we are not immune: our individual entropies are low at birth, then at death we decay, and our molecules and atoms—the ultimate phase of disorder—disperse. Around us the mountains crumble as the stones erode; stars burn out becoming supernovas. Every process moves from order to randomness following the second law of thermodynamics. Entropy—not energy—drives the world.

"Anyhow, the math is absurdly simple." Anax stopped and picked up a stick, and in the dust he wrote $\Delta S \geq 0$. Skeeter stopped too and watched in boredom. "This is the second law of thermodynamics. Delta, the triangle symbol, stands for change, and S represents entropy. The equation states that entropy's change is always greater than or equal to zero, meaning heat can move only toward cold, never the reverse. The arrangement of those four symbols expresses the difference between past and future. In other words, that little inequality is the only expression in all of physics that describes the passing of time." He squatted and scooped a handful of dust, letting it trickle through his fingers. He shook his head in awe and looked into the distance. Skeeter shook his head too, at Anax's oddness, and stepped into the hump.

Anax threw away the stick and caught up. "We're

leaving the past behind," he said. "That's a tautolo-gous statement and therefore true."

◊ ◊ ◊

Squeezed between Scalded Creek and the train tracks lay a hardscrabble area trampled bare, mostly by the feet of children, its perimeter edging of weeds presenting the overall appearance of a monk's ton-sure. Tall stands of goldenrod and ragweed thatched the creekbank on one side. The side opposite was forested by the rough stems of giant mullein poking through the riprap of mainline ballast composing the revetment that sloped abruptly upward to the train tracks. The open space resembled a lopsided square seventy-five feet or so on a side, although perceptively its size varied according to the occupants, appearing large to small children close to ground level and shrinking proportionately as they gained height.

During wet periods, the ground turned to viscous clay; in dry times it metamorphosed into dust inter-spersed by stones lifted to the surface during winter freezes. Every March a makeshift diamond was laid out by the older boys and became the site of spontaneous softball games. Anyone hitting a foul into the fetid creek had to wade in and retrieve the ball to jeers and catcalling. On April Fool's Day the company store provided a bat and ball as gifts to the community, but gloves were an unknown luxury. Not that it mattered. By May the ball had been pummeled and dunked suffi-ciently often to become malleable to the softest hands.

It was here on an otherwise unmemorable summer

day when he gained a memory that stuck forever. There was the usual pickup game, a ritual remarkable in its egalitarianism. Instead of the regulated nine players to a side there could be any number, and anyone could participate, from grade-schoolers like them on up, even an occasional off-shift miner. It was males only. Until that day this unspoken rule had never been challenged. The girls and women had never protested. They seemed satisfied with their own interests, which did not include team sports. But this day one did care, and she said so. She might have been the only girl present, and she shouted toward the diamond, "I want to bat!"

There was momentary confusion when the pitcher stopped his motion, and the third baseman told her she was not allowed.

"Why?" she said.

"'Cause you're a girl."

"Well, hit ain't fair," she said, "and I dont like hit."

They were standing next to her, and for reasons he never understood he felt obliged to reply. Saying anything at all was out of character, but he did anyway: "I'm sorry you're a girl."

She turned partway. "You're sorry I'm a girl? You're *sorry?*"

He stammered, "I mean, I'm sorry you ain't allowed to play ball 'cause you're a girl." But his qualification went unheard. In her look was the ire of the tiger. She turned completely to face him, and as he watched stupidly her fist hit him square in the nose, dropping him to his knees. Blood spilled into the dust; miniature fireworks exploded in his eyes. She shrieked and kicked out at him as bystanders dragged her back. In his ear Jeeter urged retaliation. "You gonna let a girl beat you up? Well, are you?"

The game stopped, and everyone gathered around. He got to his feet and heard the same advice from others. "Hey, Skeeter, go kick her ass!"

His eyes were tearing, a natural response when blood suddenly blocks the lacrimal ducts, disrupting drainage through the nose and causing them to back up. Despite the tears now popping forth he was not crying because of any pain. He knew better than to look like a crybaby, especially after being punched by a girl. He said, "You caint hit a girl."

"But she hit you first!" someone said, a statement quickly reaffirmed: "You're allowed to hit girls if they hit you first!" Another voice added, "Or if you're married." In response he shook his head and walked away in a cloud of confusion and self-loathing reinforced by Jeeter's mocking words in his ear. Thereafter, he was teased for being the boy who got his ass kicked by a girl. Mary Robert Vance never spoke to him, not that they ever had been friends, but from that day forward he became invisible to her, the embodiment of her general hatred of male chauvinism.

◊ ◊ ◊

Their undermanned platoon was rewarded through a program called Stack Arms, established for Marine enlisted personnel only. They were trucked to China Beach, a few klicks north of Da Nang, for three days of mini-R & R. In the distance the Truong Son mountains rose hazy and mauve, and peace reigned. On arrival they checked weapons, ammo, and other ordnance, exchanged filthy field fatigues for new shorts and skivvies, and were let loose on the beach. The men gave up their weapons reluctantly, as if relinquishing a valued body part. A weapon, like any tool, extends behavioral space after becoming part of the body schema through training, practice, and use. Once incorporated into selfhood the brain's parietal lobe recognizes the tool's legitimacy.

Marines guarded the entire perimeter. This was the second time he had seen the open sea up close, the first having been while aboard the troop ship. They could swim, play volleyball and touch-football, or cards, or just lie around getting drunk and stoned. They slept on honest-to-god cots, shaved and showered in clean hot water, and ate all the steaks, burgers, and hot dogs they wanted. Cold beer and pop were unlimited too. Corpsmen were available to treat festering cuts and foot blisters, ass and crotch rot, and myriad other minor maladies of life in-country. There were no officers among them, just other grunts. For those few heavenly days and nights no one out-ranked anyone else. You could have your hair cut high and tight. You could take Polaroids of each other laughing on the beach, beers raised and arms around each other proving the world is a clean safe place and death is another country. If you needed to spread the evidence that life in war is heavenly you might send a postcard home, and Mother Green paid the postage.

He stood apart from it all, uncaring if he was only partly visible. It was better that way, safer. You never knew if a ghost-seer might lurk among all those men, someone who intuited the duality of your shadow and noticed Jeeter staring over your shoulder from behind. Who knew, maybe one of those cameras could reveal his smoky image.

And of course there was a chapel complete with nondenominational chaplains for those seeking spiritual relief or to lend a sympathetic ear to personal thoughts and anguish. Of their team only Weasel and Donut took advantage, and both returned subdued.

They were gathered in a circle in the shade, some sitting in chairs, others in the sand. Weasel punched open a can of beer and looked at the others. "Ain't none of you religious? I mean, don't you believe in Jesus and want to save your souls?" The abrupt juxtaposition of religion and reality had disconcerted Weasel. "If you won't believe in a higher power, what do you believe in? God was here from the start, before anything. The first four words of *Genesis* say, 'In the beginning God.' There it is, right in the Good Book on page one."

"Okay," Anax said, "I believe that in the beginning entropy was lower." He was lying on his side, one elbow crooked, the hand propping up his head. With the other hand he was absently scooping sand with a seashell.

Weasel said, "Well, I ain't sure about what you just said, but I believe that our bein in Nam has a higher purpose, like we're part of God's plan. That He meant us to be here to save the world for democracy. . . .I guess." He looked away.

◊ ◊ ◊

Journal entry Yesterday, Weasel ricocheted off the subject of determinism and God, evidently in the hope of rationalizing why we find ourselves in this senseless, stupid war. I was inclined to offer a more extensive rejoinder but instead held back, realizing I had not considered his comment sufficiently to understand it myself. This posting is an attempt to remedy that personal deficiency through brief statements from the perspectives of philosophy, neuroscience, and quantum physics. I emphasize that they are *very* brief, the issue having been debated by philosophers and theologians since antiquity. I am neither. This exiguous entry in a personal journal, perhaps never to be seen by other eyes, is not intended to advance knowledge but merely anchor my thinking here in this miserable place.

Start from the premise that determinism exists and attempt to falsify it with the limitation that the future can affect the present only to the extent that part of the future is already settled and therefore inherent in the present. The New Zealand philosopher and logician Arthur Prior dissected the concept of determinism and assessed its truth value. He reasoned that if it exists then by definition events are preordained, and the number of alternative actions available in a given situation is limited. Furthermore, the action that can be performed is the action that *is* performed, by default the most favorable by being the only one possible. No matter the nature of that action, completing it satisfies our duty.

Conversely, Prior argued, if determinism does not exist then several choices are available in a given situation, not just one. However, there is no assurance that any is superior because agents in addition to ourselves are also free to make decisions, unless everyone declines the option of free-will. Thus, if determinism is true, what we do is simply our duty. If it is false then we have no duty.

Maybe free-will is an illusion, and determinism is the way of the world. Electrical potential in the brain builds before an event. The brain's neurons light up split-seconds before the decision to move a finger or cross a leg has been effected; that is, *prior to conscious decision.* The act of movement is thus a *post hoc* event because the brain anticipates the body's response, suggesting that an act or thought is secondary and therefore deterministic. Is deciding to raise a rifle to your shoulder an act of free-will or the inevitable result of neuronal discharges that precede it? If the activation of neurons not just underlies but drives all our experiences—thoughts, dreams, plans, memories—is not everything deterministic? If so, how can there be free-will?

Last, the view from quantum physics. Identical quanta behave differently, and subatomic interactions are stochastic, not deterministic. Our world presents an illusion of stability and determinism only because interactions in a microcosm succumb to averages, and the ebbs and flows outside the statistical range of normality are invisible from our macroscopic perspective. Even if we knew everything about the past with total accuracy we still could not predict the future. Heisenberg had shown this in his Uncertainty Principle, debunking Laplace's idea that with complete information about an object's location and momentum its future configurations could be predicted. The error was not in the conclusion, Heisenberg argued, but in the premiss. Thus, the historical "proof" against free-will, as argued from the comfortable armchair of classical physics, had disintegrated in the face of quantum theory. That earlier argument held that the laws of physics are deterministic. Nonetheless, any conclusion that free-will exists seems doubtful, if for no reason other than the constraint of entropy, with which it is incompatible.

And God. . . .Is He actually there? It has been said that the difference between a god and a deity is that a god creates then sticks around to nurture and curate his creations; a deity moves on after the thrill of creation passes, abandoning further obligation to the creatures just breathed into life. Our western God seems more like a deity. I hold with Baudrillard's assessment. He asks, what if God never existed except as a simulacrum? Suppose God has simulated Himself and disappeared into His own simulacrum? Do we declare the "divine referential" dead? If a supreme being can be simulated then the system based on its worship is reduced to a circular argument, a begged question of ontology. Weasel was struggling with who we are and why we are here. The answer to the first ponderable is not knowable; perhaps more accurately, the question is unanswerable. So, who are we? No one. As to the second question the novelist Charles Bukowski proposes that we have been put on Earth to drink beer, probably as valid a speculation as any.

◊ ◊ ◊

Movies were shown after dark at China Beach, although not all were selected just for entertainment. Occasional efforts were made to impart lessons on the belief that to varying degrees film can correlate positively with reality. This could be true, but simultaneously film reveals absolute correlation with itself, and in this self-emulation it reflects the essence of hyperreality, an artificial state that has neither origin nor reality.

The feature film was introduced by a short, stocky, red-faced major wearing a fruit salad that extended nearly to his waist. He strode back and forth across the stage holding a microphone, the cord retrieved or let out as necessary by a harried PFC. Personnel turnover was rapid, so he gave the same speech each night. He told how glad he was to host them, how proud the higher-highers were of the Corps' collective successes. He noted that the first U.S. troops in Vietnam comprised 3,500 Marine brothers who waded ashore at this very place at 0903 hours on March 8, 1965. Indeed, that had been a proud moment, and they—the ones who came after—would do well to savor it.

The film that night would be William Golding's *Lord of the Flies,* and it contained an important and relevant moral lesson, namely, how the people of Vietnam and similar undeveloped countries are childlike, lacking the maturity and reasoning capacity of advanced civilizations like the U.S. Without direction and supervision they regress inevitably to savagery and paganism, the same as children. Clearly, the U.S. mission was not merely to aid the South Vietnamese against the North's hegemony, but to teach its citizens the values and morals of the West and hope they stuck.

He watched the movie, but its scenes were disrupted and eventually subsumed by unpleasant memories from childhood. Every playground is a miniature battlefield where hierarchies are established and the emotional pain inflicted can last a lifetime. To adults, these outwardly harmless skirmishes appear amusing and irrelevant, mere childish play, but the origins emanate from a darker place, an inherent need to embrace tribalism and exclude the Other, those unlike us: unfamiliar, inferior, and vaguely frightening. Through every city neighborhood or small town flows a hidden river of hostility and insecurity. Those not of the immediate tribe constitute the Other and are eyed with suspicion. Simultaneously, from within the tribe an endless internecine struggle for dominance and influence plays out. Unsurprisingly, children bullied within their own group join with their tormentors to bully strangers and by excluding them feel the paradoxical pleasure and satisfaction of inclusion.

That first night of R & R they sat on the steps outside the barracks or sprawled shirtless and shoeless in the sand, drinking and smoking and bullshitting. He could see Donut standing off to the side, body slumped and ghostly white in the moonlight, resembling a scoop of melting ice cream. Donut had once been fat all over, but the training and hard time in-country had shrunk his upper body and legs while the belly roll stubbornly remained, sinking inexorably over his belt.

He sat slightly apart burdened by thoughts of Scalded Creek, not participating in the conversation but accepting the joint handed him and passing it along, getting up occasionally to fetch another beer. Marines wandered past in different states of intoxication, sometimes joining their group temporarily then moving on. Barnes was regaling everyone with the story of how he got reinstated to active duty, embellishing his interview with the battle-worn major at Lejeune.

◊ ◊ ◊

Ray-Ban stumbled to his feet. "I see a coupla dark faces out there. Speak, my brothers! Don't be shy if you think you ain't *so-phis-to-ca-ted*, 'cause none of these other motherfuckers is neither! They just crackers and fuckups.

"Wanna talk style? Let me tell you 'bout Harlem nights, what I be missin by hangin wid you grunt motherfuckers. Upscale downtown white chicks comin uptown to downscale Harlem in rented limos to dance inna clubs wid Black hep-cats. They step onna sidewalks flashin leg and spike heels, gigglin and thinkin they baaaad, soundin like a flock of birds let out a cage. College boys comin uptown to ogle the Black chicks, tryna catch the glance of big brown eyes and sniff dark skin smellin earthy and sweet, seein a flash of white teeth in the pulsin lights, glimpsin bare thigh as these beauties whirl and spin past the bandstand wid they dresses flyin up. Outside, sounds of the hot Harlem night: horns honkin, people shoutin hellos and stoppin to tell one another jokes and lies and troofs, sharin nips from bottles in paper bags; whores and pimps and junkies rubbin elbows wid street poets and drug dealers and hustlers of all kind; jazz filterin through the open doors of the clubs. The whole scene drippin sex and glamor, pleasure and pain, nobody realizin life is a false promise, a pawn ticket you can't redeem, a bag of shit left on the doorstep. They all actin like they won't grow old and wilt like a lapel carnation. Just one mo' drink, bartender, my liver can take it, just a last one fo' the gutter, then I be gone home to mama. You believe the carousel is turnin on'y fo' you, that time ain't passin but just goin round and round, but baby they ain't no such thing as a beautiful old hooker. That silver fox in mink, that struttin pimp in a zootsuit wid a ostrich feather in his hat, they already slidin toward a wrinkled death and don't know it." As if introducing a nightclub act, he teetered wobble-legged and pointed down languidly to the figure beside him seated in the sand. In a theatrical voice he said, "Just as they ain't such a creature in Nam as a old Marine grunt, 'less we mean Barnesie here. He gonna live fo-*evah*!" Someone gave a shrill whistle. There was applause and drunken hooting, and Ray-Ban took a bow.

◊ ◊ ◊

Journal entry Donut, Ray-Ban, and I are sitting in the sand at China Beach, drinking beer and watching the low waves break white then draw away black. Donut seems thoughtful. Finally, he tells me that he wants to go swimming but is hesitant. He speculates about being attacked by a shark. His reasoning: this is the ocean in front of us, and sharks live there.

However, their interactions with humans are rare, or so he has been told. Therefore, anyone attacked who survives has a vanishingly small chance of being bitten again. This is muddled, although I sense he believes that if only he could survive a first encounter with minimal or no damage he would be able to swim safely afterward. Statistically speaking. . .sort of. I do not have the heart to tell him that because such events are random and independent, the probability of a second attack is the same as for the first, no different from a lightning strike. Independence within this context of probability refers to insensitivity to past and future events. An outcome of red when a roulette wheel stops (eighteen of thirty-eight possibilities) or of a coin flip showing heads (one of two possibilities) is not contingent on any previous spin or flip, nor can the present results affect future ones. Even after seeing ten consecutive tails appear from ten coin flips, the probability of tails in the eleventh is still one in two, the apparent clustering having been a series of random and independent events.

Might sharks be attracted to colorful swimsuits? No, I tell him, sharks are color-blind. They see the world in black and white and varying shades of gray. And what about tigers? Do you want to swim with them too? I say playfully. No, I mean colors, like, do our cammies make us invisible to tigers? Probably not, but tigers can't see colors either. In fact, colors do not exist. Electromagnetic waves are colorless. Pigments in our eyes perceive certain wavelengths of light that our brains interpret as having color. That beautiful sunset that just left us was an illusion.

Donut has lodged quantitative thoughts in my mind. A drunken Marine staggers past and sweeps me into his movements before disappearing into the pillowy night. The "drunkard's walk" principle demonstrates that after a period of random wandering the distance from your starting point has increased by the size of your step multiplied by the square root of your number of steps.

Ray-Ban lights a joint and passes it to me. "A toke from the righteous bush?" he says. He turns toward me, and his aviator shades reflect a glint of weak starlight. How many millions of light years did it travel before arriving here? I inhale a toke and hand off to Donut. Above, the firmament explodes inside a sparkling dome. A full, effulgent moon detaches from the horizon, waxing the color of diluted blood oozing from a newly dead corpse abandoned in the rain. I have witnessed this scene, not merely imagined it. Being stoned flattens any confidence I harbor about reality until I no longer care. That, I suppose, is the point. Hello rain! says the blood. Dilute me until I am detectable only to the microbes, then let me disintegrate further into dancing subatomic particles and finally disperse. Rise higher in the night sky, moon, until you bleed out and turn slivery and etiolated and your energy dims to that of a single quantum of visible light: Planck's constant, a trillionth of the energy expended in one beat of a fly's wing.

◊ ◊ ◊

They stopped for an afternoon break, again flopping underneath the canopy of a large tree. They pulled off their boots with tired sighs and muttered bitching, then lay back and lit up, the nauseating stench of rotting feet thickening the still air. Immediately, Weasel started ragging on him.

"I seen you lookin behind yourself all mornin. Somethin followin us? Then this afternoon you was lookin down at your feet like some fool tryin not to step on sidewalk cracks, except there ain't none. Your shadow? Scared of it or somethin?"

He stuffed chaw in his mouth and turned away, ignoring the taunts.

"Leave him alone," Anax said. "Shadows might be more important than you think." He recounted the 19th century German fable of Peter Schlemihl, the man who sold his shadow to a stranger wearing a gray suit, and how without it he was jeered by schoolboys and ridiculed by his peers, and his life in general disintegrated. He mentioned that *Schlemihl* is Yiddish for "accident-prone," but on receiving no response continued with his narrative. Without its shadow, a body becomes transparent. Schlemihl's reality had been embodied in his shadow, and there too lay the nexus of his social status. Now shunned by every strata of society, Schlemihl was doomed to a nocturnal life, never again to walk in sunlight. However, he did not so much lose his shadow as sell it to the gray-suited stranger for gold, specifically, the Luck-purse of Fortunatus, a leather satchel with a drawstring that held an endless supply of double golden ducats. The stranger is the Devil in disguise. Whoever owns the purse has merely to plunge a hand into its mouth to retrieve them ten at a time.

Schlemihl found immense wealth briefly exhilarating, but his elation was soon overcome by the shame and sorrow brought about by his lack of a shadow. A year and a day later the stranger reappeared and offered to return the shadow in exchange for his immortal soul, but Schlemihl refused even though it meant relinquishing his fiancée, the lovely Mina, to his bitter enemy, a treacherous villain named Rascal. Mina's father had refused to give his daughter in marriage to a shadowless man. Thereafter, Schlemihl abandoned the Luck-purse of Fortunatus to the custody of Bendel, his faithful servant, instructing him to use the money for good works, which Bendel did. Schlemihl then left Germany for the Middle East, where he took up permanent residence in a cave. He lived in poverty, emerging periodically to roam the world while reflecting sadly on what greed had cost him.

The team stayed quiet and thoughtful throughout Anax's telling. Afterward, the silence continued undisturbed with exception of a hidden bird calling from the canopy.

Donut turned to Anax, source of all abstruse knowledge. "Anax, what's the name of that bird again?"

"It's a blue-eared barbet."

Everyone knew that Donut was a two-digit midget whose tour would end in a couple of months. When he spoke again his voice was soft. Perhaps he was counting the days left of his time in-country. "Sounds like it's saying, *re-up, re-up.*"

"In its motherfuckin dreams," said Ray-Ban. "Don't listen to it, Donut."

Barnes stood and broke the contemplative mood.

"Saddle up, ladies," he said.

◊ ◊ ◊

Journal entry Each member of our fireteam expresses—in some instances betrays—his individuality differently, but Skeeter stands out as unique and is to me the most interesting. We all have quirks, not excluding myself. Within our small group his extend deeper and are the most affective evidence that the mental disorder he bears and that I seek to identify has been nearly lifelong. By necessity, I entered the military bereft of books and papers and therefore proffer only a tentative diagnosis of Skeeter's peculiarity at this point. I believe he experiences hallucinations and takes great care to hide his condition from the rest of us, but some of the others, notably Weasel, seem to be catching on. My research materials are stashed in boxes halfway across the world, and our present setting in a tropical war zone is hardly reflective of a clinic. Nonetheless, I am inclined to believe based on preliminary observations that Skeeter suffers from autoscopy, which I shall describe when more time is available to write notes. If so, deducing the specific form is the next step. However, having never evaluated a patient with this malady and in light of our situation anything I say at this time is speculative.

Attempting to draw Skeeter out with questions about his early life have proven fruitless. I have the impression that his childhood was unhappy and traumatic, not unusual in people growing up in a brutal ignominy steeped in ignorance and poverty. I know little more of his history than he comes from a coal mining camp called Scalded Creek located in Logan County deep in the mountains of southern West Virginia. His mother is dead, and last he knew his father had been placed on disability from the mines because of black lung disease, known medically as pneumoconiosis. He will not recover. Skeeter hinted that he likely won't know if his father dies. Members of this community apparently are tight-lipped, barely literate, and he is not in touch with anyone. I sense that their father-son relationship has always been contentious, and that when the old man passes away he will not mourn.

As to other family members, he has mentioned twin paternal uncles senior to his father and about whom he seems ambivalent. His paternal grandparents were beloved, especially his "papaw" but his "mamaw" is dead. Papaw is, I take it, a renowned storyteller and a kindly, sympathetic man, which evidently his son (Skeeter's dad) is not. Skeeter seems to have been close to his mother but has few words to offer about her. When I mention siblings he becomes evasive, revealing only an identical twin named Jeeter, who is categorized 4F by the military and unfit for service because he "got his eye shot out." Only that simple statement without details. He has yet to mention the maternal side of his family. This is what I know so far.

◊ ◊ ◊

Journal entry I mentioned previously that we all have quirks, including me. Weasel is a curious sort. Many of his antics are attention-getting devices, although his questions sometimes can be intriguing, indicative of an observant nature. He recently asked why he has never heard me laugh. It was an astute question because neither has anyone else. Since childhood I have suffered from aphonogelia, a rare neurological disorder that prevents me from laughing out loud. The condition ordinarily results from a traumatic brain injury, but I have never experienced head trauma. The etiology in my case remains unknown despite numerous examinations by competent neurologists. The debility has caused me considerable social anguish over the years when strangers have marked me as distant and humorless. My capacity for mirth matches anyone's; it simply goes unexpressed. I try to compensate by smiling at the correct moment and often emitting a little grunt that I hope sounds approving. However, I long ago gave up trying to explain my disability and instead shrug off direct inquiries or answer with a *bon mot*, this time Bertolt Brecht's dictum that he who laughs has not yet heard the terrible news. Instead of being an intended distraction, it piqued Weasel's interest and led to more questions: What news? Who's whatshisname?

◊ ◊ ◊

Journal entry I have become convinced that Skeeter is a victim of autoscopic hallucinations, a rare and peculiar condition. Explanations are in order if I intend to discuss it further. The term derives from ancient Greek and means "seeing oneself." In neuroscience it refers to seeing part or all of yourself projected in extra-corporeal space. I provide here an overview of the condition. This posting is retrieved from memory of having read clinical articles on the subject, mainly in the French and German literature. The phenomenon has gained less attention in the U.K. and U.S. Having no research materials at hand, what I state is accurate only to the best of my recollection and woefully incomplete.

Autoscopy *sensu stricto* is the hallucination of seeing an image of yourself. Presently, three manifestations are recognized, each having distinct defining elements: (*1*) autoscopic hallucination, (*2*) out-of-body experience, and (*3*) heautoscopic hallucination. Unfortunately, "autoscopic hallucination" is also deployed as a general term loosely encompassing all the forms, injecting an element of confusion.

In a classic autoscopic hallucination—that is, when the term is applied only in its specific definition—the subject is confronted with a mirror image of his own face, perhaps including part of the upper torso and less commonly other parts of the body. In an out-of-body experience the subject sees himself lying prone at a lower elevation, which triggers several possible responses (e.g. fear, dread, ecstasy, amazement) along with vestibular sensations such as vertigo or a floating feeling. Heautoscopy is accompanied by the most variable and realistic hallucinations, including the famous "double," or in German, the *doppelgänger.*

A heautoscopic hallucination typically is colorless, pale, translucent, ghostlike, and with subsequent appearances comes to be seen by the subject as an object of perceptual salience. Heautoscopy differs from the other two forms in important respects, starting with added realism by the image not being mirror-reversed. Therefore, unlike in autoscopy it is not a "mirror image" of oneself in which the left arm seen reflected appears as the right, and vice versa. Autoscopic and out-of-body hallucinations are silent and unimodal, having the static character of photographs. There is no interaction, just a spooky self-likeness in extra-personal space.

A heautoscopic specter appears nearly always in frontal view—that is, in homothetic perspective—but profile views have been reported, and even rear views, as depicted in René Magritte's 1937 painting titled *La reproduction interdite.* All autoscopic hallucinations are primarily visual phenomena, although in heautoscopy other sensory modes can be involved. A heautoscopic specter is dynamic and multimodal possessing auditory and haptic features enabling it to speak and touch the subject, and sometimes the subject can touch it. Subject and hallucination can read each other's minds (i.e. share thoughts) and engage in conversations. It sometimes mimics the subject's movements (echopraxia) or moves independently. Importantly, as mentioned, *the image is not mirror-reversed.* What appears to be the hallucination's right hand is indeed that hand. In short, through its realism it seems to possess agency, which has the effect of weakening the subject's own, inducing confusion in his mind as to which is real, himself or the specter.

Autoscopy (general usage) springs from psychic or neurological disorders like epilepsy, migraine, schizophrenia, severe depression, anxiety, and a panoply of lesions caused by cancers and brain trauma, particularly damage to the temporo-parietal junction (abbreviated TPJ) at the temples a bit above and forward of the ears. Someone plagued by autoscopy is truly a victim to whom the association can be frightening, unnerving, or merely irritating, but rarely benign and never pleasant. The specter often possesses its own personality, allowing it to be friendly or adversarial, kind and generous or cruel and spiteful, further adding to its aura of reality. In addition, it might appear as an older or younger version of the subject and dressed differently; in rare instances it is a stranger not resembling the subject at all, in which case it is not considered a *doppelgänger.*

◊ ◊ ◊

Journal entry Am I digging too deep into Skeeter's panoply of maladies and unearthing what seem to be phantoms of phantoms? In the danger and discomfort of our situation, have I allowed myself to become obsessed? None of us is completely sane in these conditions: the chronic fatigue (our clothing is aptly named), the urge in this heat and humidity to jump into the nearest rice paddy despite knowing the risk of schistosomiasis (an analogy is venturing unprotected into a Saigon whorehouse to gain a few moments of pleasure at the cost of a lifetime of agony). On the flip side, why not? How realistic is worrying about future pain when stacked against the more immediate prospect of death or dismemberment? Saigon street vendors openly mock the notation on packets of American cigarettes by selling tee-shirts that read *Warning: Vietnam May Be Hazardous To Your Health.* We are indeed the walking dead, here or somewhere else.

Back to Skeeter. I speculate that his youth was under the pernicious crush of social invisibility. The only acknowledgment of his existence was when peers made fun of him or he was punished by his father. He passively resented his mother for not protecting him from those beatings. It was a fact and not his imagination that no one had ever praised him, told him he had done a particular task well, or otherwise acknowledged that his life might have value, that he *existed.* Not until adolescence did he capitulate to his circumstances, accept his perceived worthlessness as genuine and ineluctable, and stopped hoping to be seen as he evidently was not—a whole human being instead of an empty shell. Only Papaw treated him kindly, although Skeeter eventually realized that his own role of captive audience was nothing special: Papaw needed listeners for his stories, and anyone would have sufficed, even a casual passerby. Storytelling was Papaw's way of avoiding boredom, gaining a modicum of attention, and assuaging loneliness. And as he and Papaw grew older together, the space separating them was widening. Blame it on his increasing maturity and Papaw's encroaching dementia and diminishing eyesight brought on by nystagmus, or "miner's blindness." Papaw started forgetting things, asking him to add a back-log to the fire when he had just done so, inquiring if he knew about a particular story that he had just finished telling, losing his whittling stick when it was in his hand or on the table beside him.

I raise still another likely malady that plagues Skeeter. I believe that he occasionally succumbs to sleep paralysis. During these events, the subject experiences an inability to move when falling asleep or upon awakening. Although conscious of his surroundings he might, at the same time, undergo hallucinatory experiences. Poor Skeeter. I feel as if I am piling onto his woes and wish he would simply talk to me. I say "simply" when from his perspective revealing anything of his subjective self would entail a herculean effort that to date has proven beyond his capability.

I base this speculative notion on just a single observation. The other morning at dawn when we broke bivouac I noticed that everyone was up and active except Skeeter. He had been assigned early watch the night before, gaining an advantage of several straight hours of sleep. The claymores were being disarmed and collected, and guys were scarfing C-rats while stuffing gear into packs, but Skeeter was still lying there. I went to him and knelt. His eyes were open, the pupils not dilated. I lifted one arm, and when I let go it flopped to the ground as if not under conscious control. He whispered to me that he could not move. I called Weasel and together we stood him uncertainly on his feet. I returned to my activities and a few minutes later saw him pulling on his boots.

We are a species of storytellers, and I eventually must hear Skeeter's. The exigency of narrative is inherent in us. We need to tell stories and listen to those of others to fulfill our social contract. Given a choice between an untrue, rambling narrative and a clear and true statement stripped of plot and characterization, most people will choose to hear the unreliable narrative.

◊ ◊ ◊

It might have been the same summer that Mary Robert Vance punched him, or maybe another when they saw the BB gun for sale in the display window of the company store and asked Pa to buy it for them. They rarely requested anything, especially when he was drinking, the subject of money usually sending him into a rage. This time they took a chance. He was sitting in his chair in front of the radio smoking and drinking a beer. He sat quietly after hearing the request, lifting the beer to his lips once, twice. They waited for the eruption, prepared to run. Finally, he looked at them. "A BB gun? I dont see why not. You got to larn about guns on your own sometime."

Behind them Mama had been listening from the kitchen. "Oh Everett, I dont think hit's a good idea. They's a danger fer chillun."

Pa turned in his chair. "I dint figger you'd be hearin to the idee, so dont bother gittin het up. I say hit's done. Another word from you and I'll come in there and punch you silly. You need busy work? Git on outside and pick a mess of greens fer supper. Now, hursh your goddamn mouth and bring me another beer."

He might arrive at any moment, but often just before sleep, that hypnagogic interval of half-consciousness when the boundaries between the real and the imaginary dissolve, and dreams pause before stepping over the threshold. He might come as a visible presence, as a disembodied voice inside his head, or creep up silently in the dark on tiptoes, invisible and menacing. By now he knew the unpleasant consequences of shouting in fear, bringing their mother running and angering Pa, who then blamed him for his insomnia. This time he heard himself whisper, "I thought you was a-bed with me." He slowly opened his eyes and there he stood looking down, translucent and terrible.

"I seed you done got what we axed fer. I git to shoot hit first."

His heart began to pound. He felt the terror and shut his eyes.

◊ ◊ ◊

They got the BB gun along with a box of BBs and went to the creek to shoot it. Jeeter shot first. He aimed at a blue jay in a river birch and missed. In an unexpected act of generosity he handed over the gun and said, "Your turn." He took it eagerly and saw a chittering squirrel hopping about in a white oak. He aimed carefully and pulled the trigger slowly as Pa had shown them with the shotgun. "You got him!" Jeeter yelled, racing to the still-twitching carcass. He trailed behind, suddenly nauseous. Why had he killed it? The act had been needless. If they shot a mess of squirrels Mama could make a stew. But just one. . . .Jeeter turned toward him, eyes narrowed, a sneer on his face. "What's wrong? Hit's jist a squirrel. You feelin sick, sissy?" Before Jeeter could make a threatening move he dropped the gun and ran for home.

Pa came in later and asked how the hunting had gone. He lied and said Jeeter had shot a squirrel, that when it was his turn he had fired at a blue jay and missed. Pa asked where the gun was and wanted to see the squirrel, but he demurred.

"Where's the damn gun? I ain't gonna ax you agin, liar."

"Jeeter has hit down by the crick." He knew he had lied. He recognized the part of him who was an unreliable storyteller, although it was more. He was genuinely confused, but lacking the means to express it."

"Jeeter, huh?" Pa's fist cracked into his temple, and he fell to the floor dazed, tiny dots of pixie dust twinkling before his eyes, skull throbbing as if it might explode. He lay on his back weeping, arms crossed over his head against another blow or a kick. With a shriek Mama ran from the kitchen and knelt over him, hands fluttering like helpless moths. The sight enraged Pa, and he punched her in the head too, sending her toppling to the floor. "You done left that gun by the crick, dint you." It was not a question. "Well, fetch hit you worthless piece of shit. How many times I got to tell you how much I hate a goddamn coward. I'll beat the yaller out'n you yet or beat you to death, one." He strode into the kitchen to fetch a beer, leaving them to comfort one another.

◊ ◊ ◊

For several days he weighed the relative risks of reward and punishment. On balance, the latter greatly exceeded the former, and had he been alone in this dilemma he would have abandoned the notion entirely. It was not his nature to knowingly assume risks, nor was he inclined to strive for the endorphin rush of rewards. His preference was to be left alone, but he never had been alone.

He could not bear the itch, and after Pa went to work and Mama was occupied in the kitchen he went to the hall closet and took the BB gun. It would only be for a little while, and Pa would be gone several hours. No one would know unless another kid saw him and tattled, but why would anyone do that? Who cared if he had a BB gun?

He left the cabin, closing the door silently and walking quickly to the creek through fulvous smog from the slate dump. Locals used the creek for trash and junk disposal. Over generations it had become a museum of desolation, its displays renewed and rearranged by intermittent additions and the annual spring floods. The largest permanent item was the rusting chassis of an automobile tipped on its side. It rose abruptly from the ripples, a hulking abstract sculpture. Nearby, less dense and durable items arranged themselves artfully: a bloated mattress leaking stuffing, its springs poking through; a kitchen range; a car's battered front seat; a lone fender; the daily changing flotsam of paper, of cans and broken bottles; of toilet paper and shit from the outhouses upstream. He was standing on the bank considering likely targets when Odie Chafin happened along carrying a coffee can of earthworms and a fishing stick. They were the same age and had known each other all their lives. Odie stopped. "I see that BB gun. Hit's the one my pa's buyin off'n your pa come payday. Kin I shoot it?"

He considered. Whichever way he answered there was a chance Odie might tell his pa, who could tell Pa. "I reckon," he said. "After me." Telling him they needed a target, he instructed Odie to fetch a piece of rusty sheet metal sticking out of the mud and wedge it into the low fork of a river birch.

"Why a hunk of metal?" Odie said after he had done as asked and stepped aside. "We could shoot squirrels instead."

"I want to hyur the sound." He raised the gun, conscious of Jeeter leaning around his left shoulder to watch. He aimed and pulled the trigger. The BB hit the target with a satisfying ping, but he was unprepared for the scream that came immediately afterward. To his left Jeeter was holding a hand over one eye, blood streaming through his fingers. He dropped the gun, suddenly cold and alien, and stumbled home shivering and hyperventilating, repressing his own screams, hands over his ears trying to block the screams of this haunting Other, his hallucination.

◊ ◊ ◊

Journal entry I apologize, future reader, for perhaps bungling what I am about to say and defensively raise again the same tired excuses: the absence of research material to stiffen the spine of my statements, the dreadful climate and living conditions that divert useful thoughts into the stagnant backwater of self-pity, the constant danger of morbidity and death, and, perhaps most important, no colleague to hear and critique my ideas. For this last I scratch on the blank slate of Skeeter's mind, spouting open-ended monologues in his direction as a way or organizing what remains of my scholarly training. There are no other choices. Lacking an audience I scribble in this journal for myself; alternatively, I think of the audience as my own *doppelgänger* sequestered somewhere out of sight. So, here goes.

Certain branches of philosophy consider objects having defined—and therefore distinguishable—identities as individuals. Thus, a stone by the roadside, a baseball team, or a Marine grunt qualify equally for individuality. The fundamental particles of quantum theory, however, are excluded. Some philosophers disagree, seeing individuality as metaphysically compatible with the quantum world while recognizing that such "fundamental" objects as photons (granular particles of light) and electrons are indistinguishable one from another and therefore lack defining identities. Presumably, these are invariable throughout the Universe; that is, no photon or electron is different from any other. This caveat clearly violates Leibniz's law of the Identity of Indiscernibles, leaving the issue involving quantum particles as "underdetermined." It means that if available scientific evidence is insufficient to validate the hypothesis then subatomic particles should be excluded from possessing individuality, and the door has opened to the possibility that they are.

Why is such philosophical spitballing relevant to Skeeter's neurological issue? Because it involves identity. During a heautoscopic hallucination the subject can lose agency, the inherent sense of self that defines and reinforces individuality and allows us to make decisions in our own behalf. It can drift away embodied (figuratively speaking) in the hallucination while remaining in full view just beyond his touch. He looks at it and asks, am I one individual, or two? Conversely, by accepting the projection as a hallucination he remains within himself, and his agency stays secure. However, suppose the specter has stolen his identity and he is (literally speaking) no longer "himself." Then panic ensues. Suspecting the Other of having done this terrifies him. He might become angry and attack the hallucination or, tragically, direct the rage inward and harm himself, thinking he is the Other and the specter is real. Perhaps he believes his life is endangered because the hallucination means to kill him and gain his agency. To forestall loss of personal autonomy, the subject might stay in bed all day. This means of faking death to prevent his murder by the Other is a form of self-engulfment.

The subject can confuse the hallucination with himself if during a heautoscopic event his self-identification, self-location, and first-person perception are weak. A strong first-person makes consciousness subjective, representing itself in the act of being self-aware.

The *doppelgänger* is strangely foreign yet intimate, transcendent, and terrifying. Is it a waking dream or, as some believe, a harbinger of death? The clinical literature indeed describes cases in which a subject has killed himself, believing he is attacking the *doppelgänger*. But even if he remains passive he will wonder: will I ever be whole again or is it too late? Have I swapped identities with the *doppelgänger*, and am I now the ghost?

◊ ◊ ◊

Pa's lunch bucket clanged on the kitchen counter.
Then came his voice. "Git in hyur!"

He had heard the pickup arrive, the engine go
dead, the driver's door slam and knew Pa was about to
enter the mudroom to kick off his work shoes and dirty
clothes before coming into the kitchen in his underwear.

With foreboding he stepped into the living room
hearing Jeeter whisper, "Time to take your medicine,
chickenshit." To his left the sound of scuffling pene-
trated the kitchen door along with the metallic explosion of Pa's lunch bucket striking the floor. Then came
Mama's moans, the thuds of Pa's fists hard against her
flesh, the clatter of breaking glass as she fell against
the China cabinet.

The door flew open, and Pa stood there fully
dressed and seeming to fill the entire doorway, black
and terrible as the Gollum. Coal dust spiraling up
from his overalls rimmed his outline, forming a dark
haze against a telluric background light.

He stepped into the living room. "Dud your clothes,
boy. All of 'em. I heerd what you done this mornin,
runnin off like a yaller dog and leavin my BB gun on
the crick bank. And they's more besides. Lige Chafin
done told me what you done to his boy. I aim to larn
you good."

Mama staggered into the space just vacated. "Oh,
dont do this, Everett. He's jist a kid, not even growed
yet. I dont know what he done, but he dint mean hit."
She leaned against the doorjamb and held her bleed-
ing head in her hands.

STEPHEN SPOTTE

While Pa removed his belt he started looking furtively for possible means of escape, knowing beforehand there were no options. Bathetic pleading was hopeless, as was running for the front door. He dropped his clothes as ordered and stood naked and shivering as Pa doubled the belt and told him to turn and bend over.

Mama, unable to watch, stumbled back into the kitchen, closing the door behind her. The three licks were excruciating, stifling the shrieks of pain impossible. When it was over Pa yelled to Mama that she could come out. When she appeared he grabbed her by the hair and forced her onto the floor. "Don't never deny me punishment, woman," he said. "This here boy has got a yaller stripe down his back, and the onliest cure for a coward is by beatin hit out'n him."

They lay on the floor in each other's arms, he and Mama. He watched through his tears as her eyes swelled closed, while in his head Jeeter reminded him he was a sissy and maybe he ought to thumb over to Man and jump off the Buffalo Creek Bridge. "Ain't nobody gonna miss a shithead like yourself," he said.

◊ ◊ ◊

Journal entry One of the few scholarly items I brought to Vietnam was Valentin von Holst's modest memoir *Erfahrung aus Einer Vierzigiahrigen Neurologischen Praxis* recounting his forty years as a practicing neurologist. It retains little clinical value, having been published in 1903, but I was enjoying reading it a page or two at a time for quiet entertainment. This, however, was becoming increasingly difficult because humidity and sweat were rendering its pages more wrinkled, soggy, and less legible by the day. Ray-Ban gave it the *coup de grâce* yesterday when he snatched it from my hand and went into an insecticidal frenzy wielding it as a weapon to smash the biting flies torturing him. Afterward, dozens of smushed specimens of the taxonomic order Diptera had obliterated most of the cover, and the force of the blows that killed them had broken the spine. The volume has since been consigned to the roadside mulch. My pack has been lightened imperceptibly.

A wasp lands on my wrist. Is it a parasitoid species? An entomologist might know. Many kinds of parasitoid wasps lay eggs on caterpillars. On hatching, the larvae burrow into the host and begin consuming it from the inside. The caterpillar is turned into a zombie, not feeding, moving only when necessary, and somehow duped into protecting the invaders that are slowly killing it. I envision Skeeter's *doppelgänger* as a parasitoid wasp larva insidiously consuming his self until his being has become a shell without agency, zombified, the prisoner of his hallucination.

Imagine never having been alone starting at the earliest age of reasoning. Think of sucking in that first breath of mephitic air in the bedroom of a sparse mountain cabin closed tight in midwinter. Halitosis from rotten teeth, stink of moldy feet and unwashed bedclothes, souring of old sweat. Squeezed out like fish guts onto foul sheets to lie beside the Other, your future lifelong nemesis. Desert-dry heat from the coal stove blowing over you intent on desiccating the tender untested alveoli inside those tiny lungs, rumpled ice stuck to the insides of the window glass distorting the maple's limbs bared black against the moon.

The floorboards creak where Pa steps. We hear his hacking cough, Mama's soft whimpers. The granny woman's skirt rustles as she rises from the bedside stool and goes to the kitchen to wash her hands. She hums a hymn softly as she works the pump handle. That bedroom would someday become your shared bedroom, the bed your shared bed. Never just you, even in the outhouse when furtively masturbating or scheming how to prevaricate after committing some minor infraction, always conscious of the Other knowing it instantaneously, laughing silently as you lament his deceit, forever captious and hooting his alterity. Imagine never having a secret, every thought anticipated and judged. Imagine this, if you can, the anguish of never being alone.

Various random notions fade in and out. The shimmering heat haze makes me dizzy, slowing my steps. What if Skeeter and the rest leave me behind? Future reader, your attention, please. Feel free to consider me deranged, someone who digs futilely into the human consciousness seeking nuggets of comprehension, but whose random probes are always too shallow. Advice to others prospecting among the mind's folds: they yield only the fool's gold of speculation. In actuality, I am a poseur and intellectual cretin. What I unearth sparkles enticingly and causes fools like me to rejoice. It has appropriate structure and mass; *it could be real,* but try as I might it only masquerades as something valuable. I have other failings. I am a virgin and ask in the privacy of these pages if it matters. Should anyone care that I have yet to penetrate a woman and in this way merge my body with hers? The answer eludes my capabilities. You decide.

◊ ◊ ◊

After Mamaw died Papaw became despondent and took to hanging out in the open lean-to where firewood was stacked. He sat there whittling and chewing tobacco and taking occasional swigs from his jug of moonshine. Uncle Millard was afraid he might catch pneumonia, so he convinced Pa to join him in building a space that was warm and dry where Papaw could kill time in comfort. The two of them put up another lean-to against one outside wall of the cabin to store the wood and turned the old one into a fully enclosed shed of ten feet square heated by a Franklin stove set on a brick hearth. They constructed it using weathered boards from a spavined barn, and slabs and fall-offs scavenged from the sawmill where Millard worked that would have been burned as waste anyway. The floor was barn board, the walls barn board and batten, the roof sawmill slabs made waterproof with asphalt shingles. Pa tossed Skeeter a rusty claw hammer, and they were assigned the task of pulling nails from the old boards and pounding them straight for reuse. As a final touch, the men salvaged a door from an abandoned cabin at the edge of the camp and trimmed it to fit.

No sooner was the shed finished than Papaw gained occupancy, spending most of his waking hours inside during inclement weather or outside in good weather on the small "settin porch" he lobbied for and that was added later. In fair weather he sat there gabbing with other retirees from the mines who stopped by. They told stories, spit tobacco juice over the railing, and passed his ever-present jug.

As adolescents they sat on the floor of Papaw's shed during winter evenings while he recounted events from Hatfield family history. That first night they told Papaw they were the ones who had pulled and straightened the nails used to build his shed. He commended them on a fine job, saying there was nothing more aggravating or harder on a man's thumbs than trying to drive a crooked nail.

One of Papaw's favorite stories was how the famous Hatfield-McCoy feud started along the West Virginia-Kentucky border during Reconstruction. Head of the Hatfield clan was William Anderson "Devil Anse" Hatfield, and leader of the McCoys was Randolph "Rand'l" McCoy.

As Papaw told it, "Devil Anse was my pa and y'all's great-grandpa. He married Levicy Chafin, y'all's great-mamaw, in eighteen hunnert and sixty-one at the beginnin of the Civil War. A week later he saddled his horse, took up his rifle, and went over to Virginny to join with the Confederates, where they made him a captain. In them days all of West Virginny was part of Virginny, but I'm a-meanin the part that still is. That's whar he went. Over the years him and Levicy spawned thirteen young-uns, includin yours truly.

"And Rand'l McCoy? Warn't no moss growin on him neither. His wife's name was Sarah, but she was called 'A'nt Sallie,' and they squeezed out thirteen of they own. The two clans lived not more'n eight or nine mile apart as the crow flies, the Hatfields on the north side of the Tug Branch of the Big Sandy River in West Virginny, the McCoy's near the south bank in Kentucky. The McCoys, they joined up with the Fed'rals durin the war, but politics dint 'cause the feud. None of us has ever owned slaves or truly gived a damn who run the country, so long as we was left alone. Nope, if you kin believe hit, all the fuss started over a sow and her pigs, not over a woman, as most folks believes.

"Used to be that hogs was turned out in spring to forage on mast in the mountains. Wild fruit that fell to the ground, acorns, butternuts, pignuts and such sweetened and tenderized the meat more'n slops will do, and hit's free. The hogs growed up hairy and lean, razorbacks, they was, more wild than tame. Then at slaughterin season in late fall the clans rounded up the hogs with their pigs, separated accordin to notches cut in the ears like brands, and penned 'em up, some to be butchered, others to be wintered over.

"Well, Floyd Hatfield, who was Devil Anse's cousin, was visitin Rand'l McCoy one fall day and seed one of his own hogs with her half-growed pigs in McCoy's sty. Floyd, you see, lived on the Kentucky side of the Tug. The two argued about ownership, each claimin the mark on the sow's ear was his own cipher and cut usin his personal jackknife. A week or so later, on election day when ever'one was likkered up on moonshine, a terrible fight broke out. Three young McCoys jumped my brother Elliot and stabbed him over and over, then shot him in the back when he tried to stagger away.

"Preacher Anse Hatfield, another of Devil Anse's cousins, was also the judge in these parts and supervisor of elections. This partic'lar election was in Pike County where West Virginny residents warn't allowed to vote anyways, but Election Day was allus a sort of holiday when the clans gathered to shout the name of they candidates but also gab, picnic, drink, and fight over minor matters. With ever'one present Preacher Anse decided the time was convenient to settle the hog dispute. He picked a jury of twelve men. To be fair they was half Hatfields and half McCoys, and he said to decide amongst one another who was the rightful owner. The time was late afternoon. The jury members was drunk by then and in mean spirits so hit dint surprise nobody when they deadlocked six to six. But then a witness come forward. That would be Bill Staton, who had married a Hatfield but swore under oath he was present when Floyd cut them ear ciphers. With this evidence Preacher Anse awarded the sow and her pigs to Floyd and the Hatfields, which majorly pissed off the McCoys. Later that very day they went and tuk out they grievance on poor Elliot, who warn't doin nothin 'cept standin 'round sippin mountain dew and jawin.

"Followin the attack the Hatfields carried Elliot to our boat all bloodied up and moanin pitiful and ferried him acrost the Tug to our side, whar he died. Before shovin off Devil Anse yelled to the crowd that if Elliot was to die the McCoys was in big trouble. Soon's Elliot drawed his final breath, and even before the buryin hole was dug, Devil Anse gathered his older sons—I was too young—and some other men related to us by marriage, and went over to Kentucky and

kidnapped them three murderin McCoys. They brung
'em back to our side of the Tug, tied 'em to a paw-paw
tree, and shot 'em dead. Startin right then the feudin
was on, and matters done went straight to hell."

◊ ◊ ◊

They descend slowly toward a distant valley. Except
for their movements, their breathing and grunts, the
air has an inexpiable silence disrupted by occasional
bird calls, the soft chirps of insects from the leaf litter, the sharp whine of mosquitoes. They are far from
any road, deep in Indian Country breaking their own
trail to lessen the likelihood of triggering IEDs. Making noise is inevitable as they stumble and slide and
shove aside vegetation. Barnes walking point mutters
soft curses to himself; the rest say nothing. Exhaustion, heat, and the stress of unwanted concentration
dampen any urge to expend energy on speech. Besides,
what is there to say? Weasel has handed off his rifle
to Donut directly in front of him. Their packs weigh
eighty pounds, the Prick-25 just under twenty-five and
humping it is all the extra burden he can manage on
this treacherous ground. Next in line is Anax, and
several steps behind him Skeeter walks tail-end Charlie.

Skeeter remembers *The Shadow* radio show. They
were little kids. The Shadow is able "to cloud men's
minds" and become invisible while he tracks bad
guys. "Who knows what evil lurks in the hearts of
men?" the Shadow says. Then the cryptic, terrifying
laugh. Their favorite show, which Pa knew. It was why
he often turned the radio off just as it was aired. Then

he looked at Skeeter and said, "I dont need this horse-shit, and neither do you." This episode from memory is replaced by one more recent: left, right, left, right, left, right. . . .He tries to force his mind into a mental cadence, impossible on the sloping, slippery terrain.

He looks at a biting fly on his wrist pacing slowly among the hairs, its eyes green and goggled, wallowing placidly in the sweat. "Shoo, fly," he whispers. Miraculously, it straightens its legs and lifts off. He feels himself dissolving, the solid parts of him oozing through the pores of his skin. He imagines walking that bony road through the coal camp where drops of sweat fell into the dust before him with each footstep, leaving tiny cone-shaped craters. The thought triggers a minor ecphoric moment retrieved from his brain's left hemisphere, of antlion traps that pockmark such landscapes in the dry of summer. He and Jeeter, heat-tired and bored, caught ants that they dropped into these miniature pits of death, watching as they tried to scrabble out before the resident antlions, one to a pit, emerged in a blink to snatch them.

His own mind has become clouded by a mild delirium. He is present, and not. He turns to scan behind them and hears Jeeter say, "Now's your chance, dumbass, why dont you shoot me? Ain't got the balls, huh?" He turns and sets his feet in a muddy declivity, snaps the safety to automatic, and sprays the vegetation behind with a dozen rounds. The air seems to shatter like glass and crash in cascades. The rest of the team drops instantly and lies flat. When the reverberations stop the only sound is water dripping from leaves. No one moves. No one even twitches. No one breathes. After several minutes Barnes belly-crawls down the line to Skeeter and whispers, "What'd you see, Skeeter?"

"Dunno, Sarge," he says, now alert. "Thought I seed Charlie follerin me." His hands are shaking, and he tries to conceal them; his heart pounds, and he begins to weep in fierce retching sobs. He struggles not to hyperventilate and perhaps give himself away, make visible the inner anomic self no one has ever glimpsed, that skulking, recondite entity that is the true him. Barnes is squatting beside him. Embarrassed, he looks away and spits a stream of tobacco juice. He suspects that Barnes is wily and knows things. He wonders if he really has killed Jeeter. Suddenly, the detested image appears to his left, ghostly and leering.

Barnes stands slowly. "Okay, let's move."

Skeeter remains slumped on the ground. He feels sucked dry, as if nothing of him remains but a desiccated skin. The others turn away and start moving. They feel better, lighter, seeing their collective weaknesses sloughed onto someone else, even if he is a comrade.

Anax puts a hand on his shoulder. "Skeeter, you've got to talk to me."

Skeeter looks up. "But I caint think of what to say. Promise you won't laugh at me like Jeeter does?"

"I promise because it isn't funny. Anyway, I can't laugh. I don't know how. Ever heard me?"

"No, now that I ponder on hit. You caint laugh? Why not?'

"Never learned, I suppose. Sounds ridiculous. No one needs to learn how to laugh except people like me: the few, the not-so-proud, the weird."

"You really won't tell what we talk about?"

"Never."

"Hit'll be jist between us?"

"Yep. Just us and my journal, but no one sees my journal except me. I'll write a note inside that it becomes your property if I'm killed. In the very back is the address of a university library. I only ask that you mail it there sometime in the future. I'll already be dead if it's in your possession, you'll probably be old, the war will be long over, and no one still alive will give a shit what I've written. Here, I'll give you a hand up, then ask Barnes if we can switches places in the line."

◊ ◊ ◊

He is huge, enormous, a giant. His presence darkens the room, throws a cloud against the ceiling. Where he steps the floor trembles and squeaks as if in pain; coal dust drips from his clothes with every movement. The Gollum has arrived. He and Jeeter are small, and they look up at him in trepidation. When Pa has entered through the mudroom Mama sometimes flees to their bedroom at the end of the hall and shuts the door. She can judge his mood in an instant. Meanwhile, Jeeter puts on a brave front. He whispers, "The sumbitch caint hurt me, but he can beat your scrawny ass like a drum. Go ahead and screw up. I want to watch." If Pa has been drinking, especially whiskey or moonshine, he looks for somebody smaller and weaker to hit. Strong liquor brings out the mean in him.

The cigarettes make him cough violently in bunches. Then the hurt in his chest must be terrible.

He has taken to spitting up blood on the floor, and he groans and wheezes when the coughing finally stops. They pray for these coughing spells, he and Mama; their brief interludes allow time to escape. Pa is not particular and strikes out at the one closest, but he never sees Jeeter. Jeeter is invisible. He and Jeeter wait for one of these fits to double Pa over, then he creeps away, grabbing his coat off the hallway rack and bolting for the front door, feeling guilty and torn between hiding by the creek and staying and taking a beating to save Mama. Sometimes he returns, sacrificing himself, Jeeter inside his head telling him he must be the dumbest kid in the world. "The whole camp is about to hyur a baby bawlin right soon, and hit ain't gonna be me! Dumbbell! Stupid shit! Your ass is grass, and Pa's foot's the lawnmower!"

He has never heard a kind word from Pa nor hint of a compliment directed his way from anyone except Papaw, nothing but asperity. Neither parent has ever thanked him, deservedly or not, for stacking firewood, shoveling ashes out of the coal furnace, reaching or fetching this or that. He learned early that people seldom show appreciation for doing the expected. He had never wished for high praise, merely a smile of gratitude no matter how slight, a fleeting upturn at the corners of Pa's mouth. Mama hugged him often, and when he was still small enough to make a lap-fit she would sometimes hold him there, although never if Pa was around. Never then. In the silence she pressed her lips against his head and hummed softly, urging the vibrations along his cochlear nerves to be absorbed in the auditory cortex. Through a mother's love a child develops its sense of self; through this bond the mother erects a permeable barrier between the child and the world, allowing the horrors of reality to trickle through slowly enough to be recognized, categorized, and absorbed, and to develop the necessary mental antibodies to withstand the effects without going insane.

An episode is an experience embedded in a memory, and a memory, you could say, is an episode captured as it appears on the horizon of experience. We are equipped at birth with only the potential for episodic memory; that is, during the time preceding experiences. It develops early, first as an essence then coalescing as mnemonic precision gains traction.

Until a child reaches age eight or so the mother can buffer the raw harshness penetrating from the outside. Until then its developing imago provides a modicum of emotional protection, although sometimes the horrors slip through. Not even a loving mother can stop them all. Mothers are soft and weak in the face of crude physical power. Then they cry in sympathy and try to soothe the wounds. Everyone knows that the only permanent fix is to remove the source of that power. Easily said, not so easily done. Pa became sicker as their childhood progressed, but not sick enough to die, not until they were gone and Mama already dead in the ground. Uncle Millard advised Pa to check into the VA hospital at Logan where he could have free care and the doctors were experienced in treating black lung. Pa refused. He wanted nothing more to do with the military. He was finished with that association. The military, and the

Marine Corps especially, could go straight to hell.

◊ ◊ ◊

Journal entry In addition to heautoscopy, Skeeter suffers from a feeling of presence (FOP). This is the sensation of another person nearby, either behind or beside you. As with heautoscopy it involves a double, although with FOP the Other is invisible. Because there is no image a FOP does not fall within the category of visual hallucinations. The malady is commonly associated with persons who have been isolated for long periods but otherwise divulge no signs or symptoms of mental illness: lone sailors, explorers, and castaways, those who have spent considerable time outside the company of other people. Brain injuries also can be predisposing factors in developing FOP phenomena. Ontologically, a FOP, like a heautoscopic hallucination, involves a compromise of the agentic self through sharing it with another or even believing the self to have been usurped. A FOP has two distinct features: it is consistent in distance and location in space, and its impression on the subject is convincing and real.

I make this tentative diagnosis in Skeeter's case by observation alone; we have never spoken of it. Therefore, what he perceives during clustered episodes of looking over his left shoulder just as well could be heautoscopic hallucinations. I shall never know unless he tells me. As we were on the hump yesterday I witnessed the following sequence of behaviors. With his left hand he took a candy bar from a pocket in his fatigues, unwrapped it with his right hand, and dropped the wrapper on the ground. Still holding the unwrapped candy in his left hand he was about to take a bite of it when suddenly he glanced over his left shoulder and abruptly drew the left hand over his chest while turning slightly clockwise. The maneuver was clearly abducent as if preventing the bar from being snatched away by an invisible presence. Then he mumbled a sentence. I caught only the end, something about minding your own goddamn business. He then ate the candy and licked the fingers of his left hand. Candy in this climate quickly turns to mush. As an aside, I note here that stimulation of the anterior gyrus in a surgical setting induces a FOP.

I add the additional possibility that Skeeter might experience auditory hallucinations. These arise from the left temporo-parietal area. Sometimes the presence of this other being (visible or invisible) is so strong that the subject must stop in the midst of doing something and talk to it. Again, all is speculation until I can actually interview Skeeter and evaluate the validity and veracity of his responses.

◊ ◊ ◊

Papaw held up his right hand in front of their faces, fingers spread. "If somebody was to ax me to put this hyur hand on a Bible—a preacher, say—and name the most famous of the Hatfields I'd say my pa, Devil Anse, who knowed ever'body in these parts and was even a good friend of Gov'nor 'Windy' Wilson at one time. His name was knowed all acrost the country from newspaper stories about the Hatfield and McCoy feud, and he was feared and respected in ever' holler in this part of West Virginny and Kentucky. In Logan and Mingo counties, and I'd say north to Boone and Kanawha counties at any one time, they was prob'ly half a dozen Hatfield men called Anse that was named in his honor.

"Second to my pa would come Sid Hatfield, chief of police in the leetle town of Matewan, Mingo County, in the nineteen hunnert and twenties and a piece a-fore. Now, mind you, the Hatfields has bred many a famous person. Henry Drury Hatfield was elected West Virginny's fourteenth gov'nor in nineteen hunnert and twelve, and as a Republican, if you kin believe hit. He was a doctor and surgeon for the Norfolk and Western Railway and chief surgeon of State Hospital Number One over to Welch in McDowell County, the very town where Sid met his Maker when some murderous deppities of the Baldwin-Felts Detective Agency shot him down like a dog on the courthouse steps. Fer a time Henry Drury was even a U.S. Senator. Henry was Devil Anse's nephew, the son of his brother Elias, both of which was sons of Ephraim 'Big Eaf' Hatfield, so's I reckon that makes ol' Henry Drury my first cousin. One of them brothers, my uncles, was a rich coal operator. That would be Greenway Hatfield, and at the time of Sid's trial over to Welch fer shootin two detectives the state axed Greenway to holp choose a jury to try him! Ain't that somethin, a Hatfield goin agin his own kinfolk?

"Anyhow, the world already knowed about Sid. He was Matewan's police chief and had several nicknames, includin 'Two-Gun Sid' 'cause he wore a revolver on each hip and could shoot good with either hand. Another was 'The Terror of the Tug.' Then after he was kilt the union made a silent movie of him called *Smilin' Sid* 'cause in pitchers tuk fer the newspapers he was allus displayin his guns and smilin. Many citizens of Matewan considered him jist a thug too, no better'n the Baldwin-Felts detectives, 'cept that he tuk sides with the miners. Sid was a former miner, and in his spare time he had been a drunkard, a brawler, and a woman-izer, but one day he quit drinkin cold-turkey and give up on that life. After the nineteenth of May in nineteen hunnert and twenty the world set up on its haunches and really tuk notice. What happened was this.

"Next door in Logan County the mine operators had been able to stop the miners from a-joinin the union 'cause they had the sheriff Don Chapin and his so-called 'deppities' on the payroll, men no better'n them Baldwin-Felts scoundrels. They was only thugs fer hire too, and iff'n they warn't lawmen they'd a-been in jail they ownself, that's how on'ry they was. Why, they'd knock a hurt on a man's head, then say, 'top o' the morning' to him as he laid a-moanin on the ground.

"Sheriff Chapin run Logan County as he seed fit. As I said, he was in cahoots with the Baldwin-Felts Detec-tive Agency out of Bluefield down near the Virginny border, a strike-breakin outfit, sumbitches ever' bit as mean as his own deppities. But over to Mingo County hit was diff'rent on account of Sheriff George T. Blan-kenship and Cabell Testerman, the mayor of the town of Matewan. And a-course Sid Hatfield, Matewan's chief of police. Them three was agin the operators and sympathetic to the miners, and the operators dint like hit. By this time Sid had seed the evils of drink, as I said a-fore. He still gambled and fit some hard battles with his fists, and they say he even shot and kilt a man or two, but hit was never proved.

"That May the operators at Mingo decided hit was time to larn some miners a lesson fer tryin to be union men. That day twelve armed Baldwin-Felts deppities from Bluefield, includin Lee Felts hisself, got off'n the train at Matewan Station. Lee's brother Albert had arrived earlier, makin thirteen. They went out to the shacks whar the miners and they families lived, evicted ever'one, and throwed they earthly goods out'n in the muddy road. The plan was to do this evil job of work in time to ketch the five-fifteen train back to Bluefield. Testerman and Sid went out and watched hit happen. Jist a-fore, Testerman had telephoned the Mingo County prosecutor, who said any evictions was illegal without a warrant, which these detectives dint have, so when the mayor and Sid got out'n to whar they was and Sid told 'em to stop, they refused. Back in town Mayor Testerman rounded up some pissed-off miners and told 'em to git they guns, which they went and done. The mayor said they was to back Sid and his deppities iff'n any trouble started.

"Imagine they surprise, them Baldwin-Felts detectives, when they come happy and fat to the station to wait fer the train back to Bluefield, havin jist made folks' lives miserable. Most had already packed up they rifles and warn't carryin sidearms, but Albert and Lee Felts and another top man, C. B. Cunningham, was licensed to carry pistols in town, and they had 'em stuck in they belts. No one knowed fer sure who fahred the first shot. Some said hit was Albert Felts when he shot Testerman, who was unarmed. Others said hit was Sid shot 'em both from the doorway of the hardware store. Many was juberous about Felts killin Testerman and laid guesses on Sid instead, 'cause warn't hit odd how he married Jessie, Testerman's purty widder, 'leven days after her husband was put away under the dirt. As if folks expected her to be a grass-widder even if Testerman warn't kilt and she was to take up with Sid! None darent raised the nerve to tell Sid this, a-course.

"When the shootin started one unarmed agent hopped a passin train and got away, and another waded acrost the Tug Branch to Kentucky to keep his hide from a-gainin holes. A third saved hisself by crawlin inside a trash can and waitin 'til the fracas blowed over and hit was dark, then he waded over to Kentucky too. Later, this same feller, Bill Salter, was one of the three murderin scoundrels what shot down Sid and Ed Chambers in cold blood over to Welch. Six detectives survived the Matewan shootin and seven was kilt, includin Albert and Lee Felts. It was said that durin the shoot-out some Baldwin-Felts detectives died game, others begged fer life and was shot anyways. Also kilt was two miners and a boy loafin nearby with his hands in his pockets. When you tote 'em up 'leven died in the commotion, which lasted mebbe twenny minutes. I tell you true, that famous shootin at the O.K. Corral over to Arizona Territory had nothin on the red-mannin that day at Matewan."

◊ ◊ ◊

Journal entry We are on break from humping, Skeeter and I sitting apart from the others. I noted irregularly shaped skull depressions in both his temples, easily visible because of our Marine Corps high-and-tight haircuts. Such lesions indicate past trauma and, I suspect, derive from being punched by his father. I asked him if I could touch his head. He flinched and looked sideways at me, then said he reckoned I could. I ran my fingers over his right temple feeling the irregularities and then pushed my forefinger into an indentation. I asked him if doing this was painful. It was, he said, a little. I asked him to turn his head so I could examine the left temple. I pressed those indentations and asked how it felt, and he said about the same. The damage was old, years old. I asked him how the injuries had come about. "Pa's fists," he said, the evenness of his tone matter of fact, inevitable, as if it could be the only expected answer.

I welcome this response as a breakthrough, a tacit invitation to query him further. However, Skeeter is likely to reveal the nuances of his condition piecemeal, not in a flood. These are nuggets to be recognized and collected as they appear in my path. They also could be manifested unconsciously in gestures or in words spoken or left unspoken. I might, on an outside chance, gain enough of his trust that we actually converse, and he opens his thoughts for my inspection. Either way any findings will be based on what he tells me juxtaposed with what I see, in keeping with Einstein's dictum to include for theoretical consideration only what can be observed. Actual data would be useful, especially x-rays of Skeeter's head, although the possibility of my ever obtaining them is unlikely.

◊ ◊ ◊

Journal entry I accept the logic of the simple dichot-
omy between gods and deities discussed in an earlier
posting. That I have been sent to a foreign place and
instructed to kill people with whom I have no quarrel
is sufficient evidence that the god worshipped in western religions does not exist, which leaves a dilemma:
what sort of obligation will I feel if confronted face to
face by an enemy combatant? I have seen the aftermath of battles but never participated directly in one.
My training and accompanying indoctrination is simple: kill him. First, it is my job as a Marine; second, to
keep myself from possibly being killed. One directive
mandates duty to comrades, Corps, and country; the
second, duty to myself.

As a scientist and student of the human brain I
know this: when encountering other humans we perceive them visually as objects. If they resemble us in
general form we assume their capacity for subjective
experiences while realizing that these are not open to
our assessment. We have access only to our own inner
lives, whereas the enemy can see just my exterior, to
him an active and unitary gestalt of familiar symme-
try. He sees me, in other words, as I am unable to
see myself. Although excluded from his subjectivity,
as he is from mine, I in turn can see him in a way
that is opaque to him. I presume he has an interior
life organized and powered by the illusion of a "self,"
but am unable to see or experience it. Instead, I am

left to imagine what it must be like "being" him. The enemy loses reality if he speaks a language you do not understand. Then his death has been voiceless, and he has died in hyperreality. When confronting enemies, especially those unlike us, we deny them ontological subjectivity and deserving of empathy. Therefore, if my enemy and I perceive each other at all it will be only as appresentations. Neither is the other's alter-ego, nor do we exist in identical moments of time. His *now* is not mine. We can kill each other without guilt. So I tell myself.

Journal entry We humped all day through the heat, humidity, and stillness of the rainforest. By sunset we were exhausted with barely enough residual energy to set a perimeter, clean our weapons, wash down some C-rats with canteen water, and grab a smoke. I'm sure everyone was thinking, will it ever end? It got me pondering the nature of time and how we perceive it. Physicists know that for objects in motion time passes more slowly, a fact undetectable at walking speed. What stands between past and future? We can reprise parts of the past and anticipate the future, but between them is an interval that is neither. We think of it as *now*, or *the present*, which I alluded to without discussion at the end of the previous posting. Call it whatever you like, or what it actually is: illusion. There is no "universal time." Our illusion of "the present" has relevance only to someone else nearby. The *now* we experience would be different from an astronaut's standing on the moon. The distinction between the past and the future is phenomenological, the fact that the micro-world is invisible to us, and consequently we are unable to perceive entropy. Can the future affect the present? Only those aspects in which the future has already been determined and therefore has not yet broken free of *now*. We might speculate about protention, although the far future has not yet arrived and lacks the same reality of the past and present.

The conceptual basis of the present—the *now*—is controversial and fascinating. Conscious content is enfolded in the *now*. Our reality exists there, not in the past, which once was the present, nor in a future that has yet to be manifested. The past *was* real for its short duration as the *now*, and the future *will be* too when its fleeting moment of "nowness" arrives. Thus, the present recedes continuously in the rearview mirror becoming the past while simultaneously shifting forward into the next successive instant of the future. However, reality is more complex than indicated by a simple changing of grammatical tenses. Paradoxically, grammar is too exact to be accurate: what *is* or *will be* for me might be *has been* for you, or vice versa, because there is no universal distinction of past/present/future. They occur *in relation* to us, a concept that transcends the limits of language. Reality is therefore a description of happenings inside our individual bubbles of existence, not of things, just as every so-called "thing" in the Universe is participating in events with other so-called "things." Our realities are different, yours and mine, even as we experience what seems to be the same event.

The putative "flow" of time is the endless addition of new moments giving the sense that time moves forward toward the continuous creation of new *nows*. *Now* is the leading edge of the Big Bang speeding outward and expanding the Universe, time's moment newly unfolded and emerging from nothing. *Now* is the instant time stops and also the moment that instantiates my existence.

Agency bestows on the acting self a will that belongs to him alone, or so some believe. With agency we have potential influence only over the *now*, the past is gone, the future yet to come and largely unknown. Can the combatant take steps to preserve his existing state of entropy? In theory, perhaps, by avoiding being blown up and through that event increasing it. In other words, refrain from scattering your atoms into the cosmos. Stay instead within hearing distance of life's discordant melodies. Do not willingly enter that valley of the shadow of. . . .Good luck Anax, as if change can be delayed by wishes or inoculation.

◊ ◊ ◊

Journal entry I was too tired to finish the previous posting, so today's is a continuation. What are we, "things" or "events?" The world comprises events interacting endlessly with other events, and yet we perceive ourselves as persistent individuals essentially unchanging day to day. So, what am "I"? The answer? An entity composed of time, the central historical figure from my own past, remnants of which relentlessly invade my present. I am everything I ever was, did, thought; the sum of breezes and raindrops that brushed my skin, of memories, of words spoken and received. I consist of the narrative of my life. In brief, I am the story of myself, and in it I *exist*. Importantly, I am an entity *aware* of my existence, although like all perceptions this too veils what I truly am: a composite of events. I think of myself as living in the present, in the moment, in the time of *now*, but that notion is redundant because in what other state of time could I exist? Certainly not the past or the future. What we perceive, of course, is not the "present" at all, at least not in the sense of flowing time, which can be experienced only moment to moment, not in two moments simultaneously.

The Universe is contingent. Time is not a single entity. Nor, as I mentioned earlier, is it directional, the equations of physics not distinguishing between past and future. Time also is restless and chaotic, never being but always becoming, a network of endless events comprising not *things* but *happenings*. The distinction is important: things change, but events occur. In experiencing the illusion of time flowing we miss its granularity, its quantum halts and hops. Things are static; they persist. Events are ephemeral, fleeting. However, even the densest things are events in waiting: eventually, a stone is reduced to elements, like all matter, relinquishing its stony qualities and dissolving into quivering quantum fields. Stones seem monotonous only when we consider them as things instead of events. Picture a stone far enough into the future and it suddenly becomes more interesting.

The sun moves in its orbits, stars tumble across

the night sky. Their movements seem genuine, but it is Earth and ourselves in motion; the galaxies hang at fixed coordinates. Everything is an event in progress: my boots and pack and corporeal self, the trees and the dust and my fellow team members, all—or every-*thing*—emergent objects from a quantum universe devoid of such crude agglomerations. At the quantum level nothing resembling me or these other objects exists or could exist. And time? It emerged from a world without time, of time out of time. Our macroscopic state and resultant blurring of the subatomic world give these objects—these *things*—the illusion of reality. At the quantum level the sum of all possible configurations for that fleeting scene is its entropy. This very blurring—quantum indeterminacy—establishes time, and the fact of the blurring speaks to our ignorance of being unable to "see" the quantum world happening. Although entropy transcends vision, the smell of its invidious presence lingers. To the living, entropy has the stink of death.

We perceive nature from the scale of human perspective. Shrink a Marine grunt to quantum size and his world will blur to a fog comprising a maelstrom of spinning atoms and electrons in perpetual motion. The rice paddy by the roadside will have disappeared, the surface of any liquid vanishing at the atomic level.

On a more extended time scale consider that within two generations the Vietnam War will have been transformed into myth. Some who survived it will be alive, memories diminished to pulses of retrograde amnesia expressed as reminiscences. Historians, many not yet born when the war began, will try to assess events objectively using a retrograde method of their own, namely symptomatic assessment. However, the problem with interpreting historical evidence within the context of its times is that history was once immediate; it was *now*, passing far quicker than the blink of an eye. Future reader, after taking in this last sentence, pause. Is it still *now*? Of course. *Now* is dynamic, always moving, maintaining its position separating past from future. It is racing along at one second per second. Some physicists believe that time is generated continuously at this speed, and the newly created time is always *now*.

Can the arrow of time be reversed? Can the archer turn the bow toward herself, and would not the arrow by necessity pass through her standing in the present on its way into the past? Time's arrow moves only forward, although some claim it can circle back during the reprising of memories, a seemingly false hypothesis. Time past is different from time passing, and memories can never recapture the ephemeral *now*, which happens only once. Nor does time hold still for examination. To reverse time's arrow a memory would need to be a perfect replica of a moment from the past, in addition to relinquishing its status as memory and actually becoming that past moment. The experiencing observer would have to be at two locations in time simultaneously—one in the past, the other in the present—or be divisible into two equal and identical "selves."

As a repository of an archived event, a memory is analogous to a movie stored on film. Events on the screen move forward as if in real time, but reprising them only makes the act of viewing the film shift forward in step with time's arrow. Events in the film, in the manner of memories, stay frozen in time, receding ever further into the past. Perfect remembrance requires erasing time and in the process annihilating the self. Think about it: anyone capable of perfectly reconstructing all the events of a day can do so only by relinquishing the same amount of time from the present by not experiencing it.

Roland Barthes recognized how for a mere instant the past was the present, and that much of the present is uneventful and unworthy of exaltation. As he wrote in *Mythologies*, everyday culture is "myth" we fail to perceive. Nothing about it is cryptic, leaving the bulk of life commonplace. Human culture distracts and diverts our attention; it muddies the sense of linearity, sending episodic memory off in endless loops and dropping us at locations that have no relevance but remain somehow resonant. The thoughts of future historians will not be those of persons like us mired deep in this war. Their fears will be different, although ours were no less relevant.

Heraclitus said that no man steps in the same river twice, for it is not the same river and he is not the same man. And that is why we can never go home again, at least not to the *same* home, because home will have changed, and so will we. It is to the war veteran's great sorrow that the *nows* of his battles have become history. Then again, they were history even as he fought them. Is it possible that someone could experience multiple *nows* simultaneously? Not logically. That would require a single individual to possess multiple "selves."

Those who emerge from battle are unable to explain their experiences using the inadequate language of reductive description. As an example, we perceive more colors than we can name. Emotion-charged memories, like perceptions, are felt along a continuum, eventually fading to the ineffable. Veterans feel camaraderie because explanation of the inexplicable is unnecessary. They were *there*, and to understand what happened to them you had to be there too. Confirmation of memories requires witnesses. How do you describe to the congenitally deaf the nuances of a violin solo, to those with congenital blindness the shifting hues and shades of green inside a rainforest, to someone born without arms (phocomelia) the sensation of touch? To them such experiences are forever unattainable.

◊ ◊ ◊

Journal entry I have tentatively figured out the neurological etiology of Skeeter's heautoscopic hallucinations. Anyway, I think so, although what I offer here is hardly a firm diagnosis. The damage to Skeeter's skull seems confined to the temple areas, as I discovered earlier by palpation and so noted in an earlier posting. These damaged places are bilateral, located just above and anterior of the ears in a region of the brain known as the temporo-parietal junction (abbreviated TPJ), as mentioned earlier.

Neuroscience is progressing rapidly, but last I knew the TPJ integrates multisensory functions, making them available to reinforce the feeling of agency that allows us to create, develop, and curate personal thoughts and actions; in other words, to think and act as *individual selves*. From the TPJ arises this notion of our uniqueness, the ontological subjectivity we identify as first-person singular, allowing me to believe that I alone can claim to be *me*, that I am one-of-a-kind. In having this capacity to identify the self the TPJ naturally commands the self-Other distinction, along with recognition of physical location. Thus, in recognizing *me* it can distinguish myself from everyone else, and it places *me* in a physical location that I alone occupy at any given instant. Injuries to the TPJ from repeated heavy blows by a fist could cause episodic paroxysmal dysfunction when the subject experiences a moment of debilitated consciousness. The result can be an autoscopic phenomenological event.

◊ ◊ ◊

He dreamed of Jeeter's face, not his ghostly face, his real one, and the face had only one eye, the socket of the damaged one filled with viscous mush, wobbly and hyaline, like the guts of a newly eviscerated chicken. Jeeter's hand came up slowly until it covered that side of his face, the same substance oozing between his fingers. Jeeter sobbed quietly, barely audible huffs of sadness. "You bastard! You done shot out my eye!" The scene faded in and out, replaced by a series of photographic images of Jeeter's head in frontal view tilted upward and down, then in profile. He seemed to be posing, an evil smile frozen on his lips. He must have said something aloud and awoke suddenly to being shaken and Barnes whispering urgently in his ear, "For chrissakes, Skeeter, we're on bivouac! Shut the fuck up!"

◊ ◊ ◊

Journal entry Back at base and a chance to catch up on journal entries. Skeeter and I are on hesitant conversational terms. The path to this point has been long and arduous. I have listened carefully to his dialect and its inflections and am beginning to unravel meaning. They reveal the elisions, word choice, and cadence of a strange poetry.

Everyone has taken field showers and then shaved, filling his helmet with hot water and using it as a sink to slosh the razor and splash off the soap. Clean fatigues, or at least clean*er*, some hot chow and real coffee brewed in a pot. And best of all, a bunk! Amazing how a few primitive amenities juice up morale. Cigarettes, chewing tobacco, cigars, snuff, nicotine in any form freely available and an end to smoking curfews after dark.

Skeeter was almost talkative. I heard about his Uncle Millard for the first time, which fills important gaps in my understanding of his childhood and might offer insight into the heautoscopic hallucinations he experiences. Maybe autoscopic phenomena are a family trait, although I am unaware of their transference by genetic means. At any rate, when Skeeter was still quite young—pre-adolescent is all I can gather— Uncle Millard revealed to him something strange yet completely familiar: when he looked in the mirror to shave he saw not just his own image but someone resembling him gazing from behind and over his left shoulder. Millard, as everyone knew, had a twin named Willard who died when a child and is buried in the Hatfield corner of the Scalded Creek cemetery. No one ever mentioned his name, although his existence was scarcely a secret.

Skeeter told me other things, which I interpret as follows. School had been a struggle. He gravitated toward the practical, shoving aside abstractions and supplanting the manipulation of symbols with what could be achieved using hands and eyes. He found conceptual thinking elusive and unnerving, feeling comfortable only in his shop courses, woodworking and auto repair. To these endeavors he gave full attention. He could picture himself making repairs to his own cabin, if someday he was lucky enough to acquire one. It would be satisfying to see his burgeoning skills in action, maybe building a heated hangout for Pa in his old age, as Pa and Uncle Millard had done for Papaw, a private place of his own where he could whittle by a fire while telling stories to his grandchildren. And although union wages and benefits for miners undeniably were good, he considered he might be happier owning a small auto repair business instead. Coal mining had given Papaw nystagmus and taken away his sight; it had bestowed on Pa black lung and a lifetime of anger. This alternative could be a good life: putzing around changing oil and air filters, adjusting carburetors, repairing blown tires. No shiftwork and weekends off. It would be just them, maybe bring on a third parttime for heavy jobs such as replacing trannies and moving engine blocks, tasks too much for two men, especially when one is an unreliable haint sometimes going days without showing himself while still buzzing in his ear like an unsettling and threatening insect.

He confessed he had shot a rabbit once, "But only a few pellets hit him. He laid on the ground kickin his feet and makin loud shrieks almost like a human baby that's hurtin, and the sound got in my earholes and made my backbone tingle, almost like when you bang the funny bone in your elbow. And Pa smacked me upside the head fer being yaller." It was dark. I could not see his face, but sensed he had turned away.

◊ ◊ ◊

Journal entry This is the story Skeeter told. As a child he had gone to Millard's cabin one afternoon to deliver a casserole his mother had made. Millard, a bachelor, lacked basic domestic skills, one being cooking. This was something his mother did occasionally from kindness and concern when she was certain her husband would not find out. He surely would have disapproved.

Millard had seemed disturbed and distracted. He took Skeeter to the bathroom and told him to stand on the stool behind him and look over his right shoulder at the mirror and tell him what he saw. Skeeter replied that he saw the two of them. Millard asked if there was anyone else, maybe looking over his other shoulder, and Skeeter answered in the negative.

Skeeter remembered his uncle saying something

like, "Well, I'll be goddamn. Maybe I'm a-goin looney like ol' Papaw. He tells me he sees two of you."

Then Skeeter said, "That's Jeeter. I see him fer true. Papaw's eyes ain't so good, but he kin hear Jeeter plain enough. Maybe this other feller in that thar mirror-glass is Uncle Willard." Millard acknowledged the possibility because the opposite strap of his overalls was hanging loose.

He showed Skeeter a shaving nick. He touched it as they continued facing the mirror and said, "See hyur, hit seems to be on my right cheek. Say hit's so." Skeeter said he guessed it was, wondering if this was some kind of test. "Well, his uncle said, I'm a-lookin at this other feller dreckly. He's a-lookin back at ourself—that'd be you and me—from over my other shoulder, and I'll be damned if he dont have the same shavin nick, 'cept hit's on his left cheek jist like the real one on me, as iff'n I was to turn and look at you." Which he did, and Skeeter got his point.

Uncle Millard shook his head and stepped away. Thereafter, he let his beard grow and to Skeeter's knowledge has not shaved since. When the beard gets too thick and cumbersome he cuts it shorter using scissors. When Skeeter once asked Uncle Millard whether he still saw his brother he replied that he does, or someone like him, once in a while, but that he sees him every time he peeks in a mirror, and that was too often. This consistency must have spooked him because one day as Skeeter was passing his uncle's cabin he noticed the bathroom mirror in the trashcan.

◊ ◊ ◊

He had delayed showering and shaving because Anax wanted to talk, so he told the story of Uncle Millard's hallucination, which afterward Anax said probably was heautoscopic in origin. He was lathered up and staring into his shaving mirror not just at his own face but another's, a separate presence standing behind him also with a lathered face and head bent forward. It was familiar, resembling him, sometimes momentarily supplanting him. It might mock him, scowling when he smiled, smiling when he scowled. Other times it mimicked him, eerily anticipating with perfect timing tiny facial tics made purposely: a slight lift of the eyebrow, a quick forward lean to examine a front tooth, starting to comb his hair but hesitating with arms raised and comb in hand. And never was this Other's reflection mirror-reversed. The same as Millard's hallucination.

He stood before the mirror and looked at the hand holding the razor, his right hand. In the reflection it appeared to be his left. This was the mirror-reversal effect Anax had explained. As a test he lifted his right hand and moved it forward until the razor touched the glass, confirming that his real self was directly in front, although still appearing behind his other shoulder was the dimly reflected image of the Other, the hallucination he had known as Jeeter since he could remember. He too held a razor in his right hand, the right—*or not mirror-reversed*—hand. Anax had tried explaining that during a heautoscopic hallucination the projection appears in extra-personal space dissociated from the body and is *not* a mirror-reversal. It was complicated, but he was starting to understand. The body and the self are fused during these episodes, and the projection is a left/right reversed mirror image of the subject's body, just like his own was at that moment.

◊ ◊ ◊

Journal entry I am sensing that Skeeter is on the threshold of understanding at least the rudiments of his condition. The issue, however, extends deeper. Suppose you stepped through the mirror and looked back at its nonreflective surface? Would doing so reveal whether your reality is indeed a simulacrum? Probably not. In the absence of a mirrored surface the reflection of your *doppelgänger* will have vanished. Perhaps a version of hyperreality slips through the transparency of phenomenal selfhood and presents an unforeseen experience masquerading as your personal version of reality. In originally manifesting its illusion hyperreality erases certain phenomenological road signs, similar to how the illusion of "reversal" in a mirror does not reverse either left and right or up and down; rather, the reversal occurs in the direction of the axes perpendicular to the mirror's surface. The appearance of a reversed image is psychological, not an optical effect. What does Skeeter see? Who is it that looks back? He must feel like Ireneo Funes, protagonist in the Borges story "Funes, The Memorious" whose fall from a horse crippled him, but also knocked his brain askance, banishing recollection to a peculiar obscurity and leaving him eternally surprised on seeing his face in a mirror or examining his own hands, now those of a stranger. Which is it who plots to obfuscate, himself or his image?

The metamorphosis of reality into hyperreality, those models of a real world not anchored in reality, occurs at the instant the real becomes confused with the model. Then like our illusion of reality it too becomes transparent to the phenomenal selfhood. Without being aware, the viewer's perception of reality has been reversed imperceptibly. If sitting in his living room the television now watches *him*; the event onscreen is not happening elsewhere because *he* is the event. The medium is information defined as *him*, and so is the message. Our war here in Vietnam exists in the hyperreal. Hippiedom, its putative antithesis, is transfixed by the individual as performance art. As a social movement it dimly recognizes the danger of hyperreality, and its desperate attempt to escape back to reality, as Baudrillard says, has become *vérité*.

We live in a time of semantic and optical confusion. The war here is transmitted back to the World as pictures. The photographic image is itself a hyperreal object, a nostalgic grasp at history. It lacks authenticity because it can be reproduced endlessly, and because an original does not exist. Similarly, future reader, the body bags shown on the evening news, presuming you were watching, accumulate in hyperreality. They appear in the same fever dreams as cloned objects, photographic reproductions, Andy Warhol's soup cans, the human form's demise conceived as Marshall McLuhan's message devoured and excreted by the news media and treated by the military as data. And why not? A series of body bags, in the manner of photographs, has an eerie sameness. I know. I have seen them carefully aligned in rows to be shipped like cargo back to the World. We have changed the way progress in war is measured, substituting enemy body counts for territory won. Is it a real war, a facsimile, or merely a coincidental display of underlying quantum events? Back in the World television delivers the war in timed sound bites, and the illusion of rhythmic temporality is now pervasive: when a former colleague authored a statistics text he dedicated it to his mother, who had wondered aloud why the evening news lasts exactly thirty minutes.

◊ ◊ ◊

Journal entry This morning as we broke bivouac I overheard Barnes and Skeeter talking, Barnes curious as to whether Skeeter's father was at the battle of Chosin Reservoir. Skeeter said something like, "I dont recollect he ever said where he was."

I looked up and could tell from their mutual body language that Barnes was embarrassed for asking, Skeeter no less so for having been asked. They looked away in opposite directions and spit streams of tobacco juice.

"I'm from Pike County, Kentucky, jist acrost the Tug Branch from Mingo County on your side," Barnes said. "I've knowed some Hatfields from 'round thar."

"They's Hatfields all through them mountains," Skeeter said, "though I dont recollect no Barneses."

"Did your pa come back wounded?"

"Iff'n you count bein short some toes and fingers.

I caint say how many of each 'cause I never counted 'em up. I kin tell you he had enough fingers to grip the neck on a likker bottle." Skeeter then started packing his gear, signaling an end to the interview.

◊ ◊ ◊

Journal entry I have been trying to remember details of my reading on autoscopic phenomena, specifically, what the subject feels when confronting a heauto-scopic hallucination. Mark this as another time when I greatly miss my collection of journal articles. But complaining will not do any good, so onward!

The state overall when confronting the *doppelgänger* is dreamlike, a feeling of detachment of self from body. This is accompanied by a feeling of depersonalization, even fear that some inherent and vital component has departed. Accompanying these sensations are distur-bances of kinesthetic equilibrium and awareness.

To state this differently, when experiencing a heau-toscopic hallucination the subject becomes immersed in a parallel model of reality. However, the level of the hallucination's verisimilitude depends on his perception of the event and subsequent reaction to it, less so on the specter's characteristics. Bouts of echopraxia might arise in the midst of a heautoscopic episode during which the specter mimics the subject's movements in real time, anticipating them perfectly, or mimics his words or thoughts. Having his inten-tions anticipated extends to the specter a degree of autonomy, threatening and disturbing the subject's sense of agency. The subject understands that the hallucination has invaded his mind, and the two might exchange thoughts. The specter's manner could be friendly or unpleasant, attentive or aloof, agreeable or argumentative, accommodating or critical and judgmental. If subject and specter ever touch, the latter feels corpselike, cold and lifeless. Importantly, the subject might reach a tipping point, unable to distinguish himself from the specter, uncertain which is real. Ontological subjectivity manifested as a weak ego heightens his risk of losing agency completely— and thus himself—to the *doppelgänger*. I must reduce these and other thoughts to a list of straightforward question with which to query Skeeter. I add that this malady of his has become a major distraction. I am neglecting other unrelated observations and attending poorly to my objective for being here.

◊ ◊ ◊

Journal entry Barnes mentioned casually that he can smell gooks and knows if any are in the vicinity. Future reader, listen up, as we say in the military. I present Barnes' words to me here in the Appalachian dialect he and Skeeter use so fluently. If not exact, they are close enough. "Hit's the goddamn truth, Anax, I kin smell 'em. They was so many Chinamen spillin over that ridge at the Chosin that by mornin when they cleared out the whole top of the mountain stunk of garlic. Around hyur hit smells like rotten fish sauce iff'n they's gooks in the area. I swear to God." He grinned and raised his right hand, first three fingers pointed up in the Boy Scout salute.

◊ ◊ ◊

Journal entry Donut is afraid of large animals. He believes tigers lurk in the forest ready to pounce on us, that crocodiles infest the rivers we wade across holding our rifles above our heads. When everyone was drunk and stoned during R & R he confessed to me the basis of this fear. He had been raised on a farm in Iowa and assumed when growing up that he would be a farmer like his father. The path seemed assured, not even worth thinking about. Then at the age of twelve he experienced an event that would alter this vocational trajectory and permanently damage his psyche. One morning after breakfast his baby sister, a toddler, had wandered unseen toward the barn and slipped between the railings of the pig stye, her little dress redolent with spilled milk and oatmeal. The family heard her screams but arrived too late. The pigs already had devoured most of her. Donut finds the eating of pork rebarbative, if not outright cannibalistic. The transmutation of his sister's flesh into the flesh of pigs hypostatizes his nightmares.

◊ ◊ ◊

When they went to visit Papaw in his shed they had to knock, then he might open the door, or not, according to his mood. He remembered one winter evening when Papaw opened his door and looked at them, and said, "What the hell does y'all want? I ain't buyin no magazine subscriptions." Then he grinned, and they knew he was joking. He stood aside and said,

"C'mon in hyur quick and set down on the floor a-fore that wind goose-pimples your hide, and I'll tell y'all 'bout the battle of Blair Mountain. Ever heered of hit?" They said no and settled in to listen. Papaw loosed a stream of ambeer into the fire making it hiss before settling back in his chair. "I was borned in nineteen hunnert and fourteen jist at the beginnin of the Great War." He paused to pick up his stick and whittling knife from the small end table beside his chair. "As y'all know, the Army dont take leetle babies." He shifted in his chair and chuckled. "By the time nineteen hunnert and twenty-one come 'round I was, well. . . .' He stopped whittling and looked at the ceiling. "Mebbe I was seven year old, or tharabouts. Still too leetle to dabble in mischief. But fer the older boys and the men they was plenty of mischief jist waitin fer 'em to pass on by. Yessir, they sure was.

"Logan and Mingo counties was the richest counties in all the U.S. of A. The richest in coal, that is, 'cause 'cept for the mine operators ever'one else around hyur was poor as a church mouse, and still is."

"Why is a church mouse poor, Papaw?" Jeeter said it, but it seemed to come out of his own mouth as if they owned just one between them.

Papaw took off his hat and scratched his head. "Goldurn iff'n I know. Prob'ly hit's 'cause church mice dont have much money. Anyhow, hit's jist a sayin, what folks tells one another when they caint think of somethin else. . . .I reckon.

"Fer years Logan County—the very place whar we live today—was run by rich men who owned the mines hereabouts. They lived in fancy houses, not cabins, and they dressed in suits sent down from New York and Philadelphia. The wives and daughters had the latest styles of clothes, such as a-wearin hats with big feathers from birds nobody from 'round hyur ever seed alive, not in Logan County, leastwise.

"To keep the mine union organizers out'n the county they had Don Chafin, a mean, dishonest sumbitch. For this dirty job of work he had his sheriff's salary and a lot more that the owners paid him under the table to crack the noggins of union organizers. He run the county as he seed fit, includin earnin a pretty penny sellin moonshine. The owners give him money to support mebbe two-hunnert deputized thugs, on'ry and crooked as him. When a bunch of miners outside the county a piece north of us went to strikin he stood a-front the courthouse at Logan Town with his men and declared that no union man would enter Logan County and live to tell the tale. Well, union men along Cabin Crick, Lens Crick, Crooked Crick, the Little Coal River, and the rest of the Kanawha Valley jist up north a ways disagreed. This was not long after the Great War ended, and lots of 'em was former soldiers.

"They started gatherin, hunnerts of 'em wearin old army uniforms and totin ever' sort of weapon you kin imagine, includin machine guns, which in them days you could buy in the comp'ny stores. They started marchin on Logan Town by way of Boone County, intendin to come over Blair Mountain, yellin how they was gonna hang Don Chafin from a sour apple tree and unionize the southern West Virginy coal fields. Blair Mountain, as y'all know, is jist a few mile from hyur, and hit's the most famous place in the county 'cause of this uprisin. Soon they was thousands of 'em marchin, these miners, and thousands more joined up along the way. They tuk to breakin into comp'ny stores where they stoled weapons and ammunition, and they forced peaceable miners to join 'em at gunpoint. They commandeered trucks and trains and threatened to shoot the drivers and engineers if they dint take 'em south. They was a hardness 'tween the two groups that led to kidnappin and torturin and all sort of shenanigans. In the end hit got to be the biggest labor uprisin in the history of the U.S. of A. Says right in the hist'ry books, or so they tells me. I reckon you young-uns kin read hit your ownself. Me, I never tuk to readin. I'm tellin the story as my pa Devil Anse told hit to us when we was your size.

"Anyhow, these miners set up camps along the route with cook tents turnin out warshtubs of beans and sassengers, coffee biled day and night. They was like a army on the move, which in actual fact they was. Gov'nor Morgan, he axed President Harding fer fed'ral troops to break up the march. That was the end of August in nineteen hunnert and twenty-one.

"The president done put out official word advisin these on'ry miners to quit the horseshit and start headin fer home by the first day of September or he'd send the army from Fort Dix in New Jersey down hyur to kick some ass. The miners ignored hit. Meantime, hunnerts of outsiders thinkin they be law abiden citizens come into Logan Town to support Sheriff Chafin agin what he told 'em was outlaws, but was truly only miners on strike a-tryin to set up a union shop. When they got too rowdy fer Sherrif Chapin to handle the gov'nor sent W. E. Eubanks, a Army colonel in the Great War, down to take charge 'cause by that time some two thousand volunteers was in the county armed and ready to defend Logan Town. Washington sent five bombers on standby, and Fort Dix was put on alert. Meantime, the two parties—miners comin from the north and Sheriff Chafin's deppities and volunteers to the south—clumb Blair Mountain and set up lines fernint to one another. The battle drug back and forth, first one side winnin then the other. You could hear the shots echo agin the mountainsides day and night. Both sides fit hard, and neither was about to yell uncle. Finally, after several days and nights a trainload of Army troops come, and peace was restored. When the dead was toted up they was fewer'n fifty, with more'n that wounded. Hit's worth mentionin that most of the strikin miners dint wear army uniforms. They identified one another by a-wearin blue bib overalls and a red bandana tied 'round they necks. Hit's whar the name 'redneck' come from, and hit's the God's truth."

◊ ◊ ◊

In Copenhagen on a winter night in 1925 Werner Heisenberg, then an acolyte of the renowned Danish physicist Niels Bohr, had an epiphany. He was just twenty-five, walking in the park behind the eponymous institute named in honor of his mentor. Around him intermittent streetlamps threw weak pools of light onto the walkway. In one of them Heisenberg saw another man out for a stroll. The partly obscured figure passed out of sight and vanished into the darkness before appearing in another pool of light, then disappearing and reappearing under different streetlamps along his trajectory. What if electrons circling in atoms did the same? It could explain Bohr's strange theory of how they jumped orbits in "quantum leaps," each time releasing a photon of light. In keeping with Einstein's admonishment to include in theories only what can be observed, Heisenberg wondered if electrons are "real" only during instants when they are observable but otherwise do not "exist." Stated differently, if during the fleeting interval between an electron's successive interactions with objects it vanishes like the man in the dark then effectively it would not "be there." Furthermore, if an electron is manifested only during an interaction—that is, when it collides with something else—then in those intervals between collisions its position is indeterminate, and the location of its next appearance can be calculated only probabilistically; in other words, by statistical inference. Thus, electrons gain reality only during these interactions and when undisturbed exist nowhere, which is not exactly the same as saying they do not exist. Rather, it means that their locations are indeterminate.

Which reminds me again of a Borges' story featuring his imaginary planet of Tlön. Suppose that on a Tuesday a man walking along a deserted road loses nine copper coins. Call him X. On Thursday, Y finds four such coins on the same road, and the next day (Friday), Z finds three more near the location where the original nine were lost and the four were found. On that same Friday X finds two coins in his house.

Are they in sum the original batch of nine? A heresiarch residing on Tlön has serious doubts. Is it reasonable, he posits, to believe that four of the coins did not exist between Tuesday and Thursday, three from Tuesday until Friday, and an additional two between Tuesday and Friday? To him, it is logical to believe they existed all along "albeit in some secret way, in a manner whose understanding is concealed from men, in every moment, in all three places." Is it possible that on Tlön at the time of Borges' writing the populace had not yet been told about quantum theory?

My destiny is uncertain, future reader. Think of me metaphorically as similar to a quantum such as a photon or electron: suppose that either my momentum or initial position can be predicted, but not both simultaneously, and my future not at all. This is Heisenberg's uncertainty principle. Using imagination and taking a few metaphorical liberties it can be applied equally to subatomic particles and macroscopic life. Momentum is obtained by multiplying the velocity of a quantum by its mass. Velocity measures both an object's direction and its speed. Momentum, in depending on velocity, does not have direction. Position then must be determined in a separate calculation. My position changes with each step and gesture, each breath and heartbeat.

If you already knew the substance of this posting you will not be enlightened. Perhaps the information is new, and you find it boring or are too pressed for time to ponder what for you are novel ideas requiring a different way of thinking. If you are that person, future reader, I pity you. Contemplation is a species of action. Words and equations have inherent meaning and beauty. They separate us from the insects. Convince yourself that time is illusion, and you can read and think languidly. Passing up these supreme pleasures without pausing to savor their scents and flavors renders your existence improvident and lessens your humanity.

◊ ◊ ◊

Journal entry We reproduce zoo animals from captive parents and retain the young in confinement for a lifetime. These specimens are not ontologically real; rather, they are phantoms, second-order simulacrums. Why not follow the Spartan way of taking male babies from their mothers and raising them to manhood in barracks? These men then lived lives loosely imprisoned except when undergoing military training and participating in wars. The Spartans fostered sodality; so does the Marine Corps. Brotherhood demands forced responsibility, a special form of imprisonment while retaining the illusion of freedom. We buy into it, so why not this too? Because many would consider the Spartan method of rearing future warriors in captivity to be cruel, unethical, pathetic. Zoo animals, not so much. Their function is to entertain us. Animals are truly pathetic only when their lives mingle with ours. Otherwise, they have lives apart from ours, often cruel and unethical if held to human "civilized" standards, although doubtfully pathetic until we judge them. Are they capable of pathos? Some are. Left alone, all animals have species-specific means of dealing with morbidity and mortality, a relative few in sentient ways, the overwhelming majority indifferently.

What distinguishes our wars are "rules" devised to render them ethical. These have been written down, the language arranged in legal context, the content mutually agreed upon in treaties and conventions, what you would expect from an advanced life-form with the intellect to define "sentient." After the documents have been signed and stamped and the group photos taken we can kill each other legally, even "ethically." Never mind that the result is always pathetic.

◊ ◊ ◊

Unlike some, they never strived to be cynosures or went looking for fights, but neither were they pacifists. They simply went along, inseparable, stumbling through mindless pre-adolescence in a Ptolemaic universe where Scalded Creek hovered at the center and all else paled outward to eventual nothingness. Charleston, the capital seventy-five miles to the north, might as well have been part of the Milky Way. Maybe that was why events in the aftermath of finding the fishing lure seemed so normal.

It was a sweltering day in August. Mama was hanging out the wash and sighing. Pa, off shift, was drinking beer on the shaded porch with his older brother Millard. There was no ice to be had at the company store and no room in the fridge, so the bottles were chilling as best they could in a bucket of pump water.

The two of them were barefoot and shirtless, wearing only bib overalls. They ambled along the shady path that followed the contours of Scalded Creek, kicking up dust and stopping occasionally to examine an insect or unusual stone, anything to assuage the boredom. The creek was low in the dry season. The few creatures able to survive in its water turned black and acidic by the tipple's effluent had gathered in the deeper pools.

They came to a familiar trail perpendicular to the creek that led deeper into the holler away from the gathering of shacks that made up the coal camp. At the trailhead was an unnamed pond fed by cold underground springs of clean water. It would feel good to shuck the clothes and take a dip, wash off the dust. Bullfrogs plopped from the bankgrass as they approached, and they silently regretted leaving their gigs behind. At least they were equipped to fish. Skeeter carried a fishing stick. It had a length of string tied to the end, and in an overall pocket was a discarded metal snuff box containing a couple of fishhooks. They never bothered carrying bait; worms and crawdads were easy to find.

They waded in, hooting at the chill and splashing one another, Jeeter shimmering translucent against the sun. He paused suddenly, a cruel sneer on his lips, and lunged at Skeeter. "I'm a-gonna drown your sorry ass! Push you down amongst the minners and catfish!"

Skeeter stumbled back, tripping over a partly submerged branch. When he came up sputtering and rubbing his eyes, Jeeter was gone. His dunking had muddied the surrounding water, but through the turbidity he could see a bright spot, something unusual a few inches beneath the surface. When he lifted the branch a green fishing lure with white spots emerged, one of its hooks embedded in the rotten wood. He pulled it free, wiped off the algae, and decided to keep it.

Even better, he decided to give it a try. Instead of a hook he tied the eye of the lure to the end of the string, which was about five feet long, and cast it in front of him, then pulled the line slowly toward himself hand over hand while squeezing the pole between his knees. Something rose upward to examine his offer, leaving a swirl on the surface. Excited, he threw the lure outward with all his strength, feeling it jerk to a stop accompanied by a sharp sting in his right temple. He had hooked himself. He looked for Jeeter but did not see him. Gingerly, he cut the string close to the lure with his jackknife and hurried home, alarmed by the blood dripping from his head.

◊ ◊ ◊

He found Mama in the yard still hanging out the laundry and ran to her crying. She spit out a clothespin and said, "My lord, child, lookit what you went and done! Oh, poor thang!" She dropped to her knees and began dabbing at the lure with the bottom of her apron. "Let's git you to Pa."

They found Pa and Uncle Millard on the back porch still drinking beer, and his mama said, "Everett, do somethin! The boy's hurt hisself!"

Pa set down his beer. He stood and shouted, "You shitbird! See what you went and done? Goddammit, I'm jist trying to enjoy my day off, and you come 'round and spoilt hit!"

Millard said, "I believe the boy's hurt, Everett. It ain't his fault. He's jist a young-un."

Pa turned on him. "Then whose is hit? Think that fishin lure jist jumped up and grabbed him by the head?" He turned back to Skeeter. "Did you steal hit?"

"No, Pa, we found hit stuck to a log, honest." His crying had diminished to sniffling.

"And who is *we*?"

"Me and Jeeter."

"Jeeter, huh? You're as looney as your papaw."

Mama was frantically wiping her hands on her apron. "Should we take him to the doctor?"

"Naw," Pa said. "I kin fix hit." He went to his truck and returned with a pair of wire cutters. "Come hyur, dumbass, and holt still." The lure had a treble hook at its tail end, but only one tine was embedded in Skeeter's scalp. Pa pushed it completely through, exposing the barb, snipped the tine off near its base, and slipped the hook out.

Skeeter howled. Pa became enraged. "You want somethin to cry about? You axed fer hit, you yaller leetle bastard!" He punched Skeeter hard in the temple where the hook had been and left him lying dazed on the porch floor. Mama gathered him close and started to weep, so Pa punched her in the head too, leaving both semi-conscious and groaning.

Millard, still seated, said, "You ought'n not to done that, Everett. Hit was downright mean and unchristian."

"Mind your bidness. You ain't got the burden of a shiftless family, so your opinion ain't worth shit." He opened a beer.

◊ ◊ ◊

He has always been the "leetle brother," the sec-
ond-born if only by minutes. Nonetheless, Jeeter often
reminds him of that inferior status. "Hit's been told
to me by folks that knows this stuff about you bein a
shit-eater. When they's two in the womb only one kin
be borned first, and the other has to wait his turn.
That's you, Skeeter. When a baby is near bein borned
he takes a big dump so's he comes out clean and dont
embarrass nobody, includin hisself, by shittin on his
mama first thing. Then he sashays on down the birth
chute and gits borned. And the one left behind? He
has to swaller that shitty water, gulp it all down, a-fore
he kin be borned in his own time. That's you, Skeeter,
ol' number two-eatin number two, Skeeter, Skeeter,
you ol' shit-eater! How's it taste, leetle brother? And
that ain't the all of hit. I'm a year older'n you. I was
borned on the last day of nineteen hunnert and for-
ty-one jist a-fore midnight, but your ugly ass warn't
seed by nobody 'til *after* midnight, makin you borned
the first day of January nineteen hunnert and for-
ty-two. What a dumbass! Why'd you wait, turdbird? We
coulda been the same age."

◊ ◊ ◊

"Kin you see Jeeter, Papaw?" He always worried that
Jeeter was extra good at hiding or could make himself invisible, like the Shadow. Somehow, Jeeter was
getting away with stuff and leaving him to face the
consequences.

"Wal, my eyes ain't too good these days. In this hyur fahrlight mostly what I kin see is shadows dancin ever'whar. Got the nystagmus, and them doctors, they tell me hit won't git no better. Ain't any medicine fer hit. The bright light hurts somethin fierce and gives me headaches, and I got hardly no night vision a-tall out'n in this hyur shed. Got to feel my way back to the cabin iff'n hit's a 'specially dark night with a young moon. You could say I'm caught 'tween the shit and the sweat. That's what the mines gits you. Iff'n the roof don't fall on your head, then the black-damp gits you. Me? I got this hyur nystagmus to show fer them years of walkin to the drift mouth of the mine and crawlin into the mountain 'cause the ceilin warn't but four or five foot high, too low fer a man to stand, and crawlin up to my "room" in the lamplight—that's the open space whar a man done his work—then drillin into the coal face with the auger, packin the hole with powder, and shootin the face, hopin you could crawl away a-fore the whole goldurn mountain fell on you."

"What happened next, Papaw?"

"Next you shoveled your tonnage from your knees into coal car a car drug by a donkey to the scales to be weighed." His shoulders sagged. "I caint see y'all, but when you and Jeeter says y'all's hyur, I believe hit. Good grandsons dont up and lie to they old papaw, does they now?"

"Nossir."

"Who said that?"

"Me, Jeeter."

"Then you, the other'n, needs to speak up."

"Yessir, Papaw. Hit's me, Skeeter. I'm hyur," he said.

"Then I reckon hit's settled, and iff'n either of y'all wants to say somethin jist open up your mouth and spit hit out."

Skeeter could not hold back. "Lemme be, goddammit!" He punched the air and rolled on the floor as if scuffling with someone.

"Now, dont be a-cussin," Papaw said.

"Pa does."

"Yeah, 'cept your pa's growed and y'all ain't."

"But he's allus a-hittin me, Jeeter is."

"You could hit him back, then mebbe he'd leave you be."

"I would, iff'n I could find him."

"Well, you young-uns jist stop hit or I'll send y'all home to bed."

"Yessir, Papaw."

◊ ◊ ◊

Journal entry Short conversation with Skeeter. I'm gradually piecing his childhood together. The family dynamics are about as I suspected: passive, abused mother, domineering and abusive father absent for nearly three years while in the military. On Saturdays during the Korean War Skeeter went to the morning matinee at the movie theater in the closest town, which is Man. Admission cost a nickel. His mother always gave him the nickel and two or three cents for penny candy. Someone from the coal camp would drive them in and pick them up. The place opened at ten, and the first showings consisted of Disney cartoons. There were two feature films, typically cowboy movies, and inserted in between was a news clip about the war lasting perhaps fifteen minutes. This was the part he waited for. His mother had heard nothing from her husband since he left for boot camp. She assumed he had been deployed to Korea, but had no actual proof. Nor did she know if he was even alive, except that if he had died a member of the military would have come to the cabin and told her. Nobody had ever come, and it was now late spring of 1951. The newsclip always showed soldiers or Marines on the march or in actual combat with lots of explosions and gunfire and narrated by a solemn voice touting the courage and hardships of these men. He tried to grab a front row seat so he could see their faces better and maybe catch a fleeting glimpse of his father underneath one of the ubiquitous helmets. Sometimes they even showed someone's face with a cigarette sticking out of his mouth, a scraggle of beard, and tired eyes. But never Pa.

◊ ◊ ◊

"This damn eye trouble has me madder'n a furriner with a bee stuck up his butt. You boys in hyur?"

"Yessir, Papaw."

"Who was that jist answered? Hit's darker'n Hell's coal cellar."

"Hit was both of us, Papaw."

"Ah, if both y'all's hyur then y'all kin both git busy a-buildin up that fahr a-fore I go all the way blind and caint do no whittlin a-tall." He fumbled in a pocket of his overalls for the whittling knife, voice diminishing to an angry mutter. "Goddamn nystagmus."

◊ ◊ ◊

He was shoving chaw into his cheek. Ray-Ban lit a cigarette and looked his way. They were on break from humping, sprawled in the shade and wringing the sweat from their bandanas and grumbling. "How come you crackers chew that shit?" Ray-Ban made a face and shook his head, baffled. "Fuckin shit is dis-gus-*tin*."

"'Cause hit makes fer a purty stain in the sink," Barnes said, spitting a stream.

"And 'cause hit's good fer killin flies," said Skeeter. "See that fly yonder?"

Ray-Ban turned partway. He nodded in the direction Skeeter was looking. "You mean the ugly motherfucker with the scary green eyes?"

"He'd be the one." Skeeter cleared his throat and loosed a nearly horizontal stream of ambeer, plastering the fly to the leaf.

"Holy shit! That sucker was, what, six, seven feet away? Get rid of yo' rifle, bubba, you don't need it. Nail dem Viet Congs 'tween the eyes wid baccy juice!"

Skeeter said, "My brother kin do ten foot. He brags and says twelve, but dont believe hit. Papaw, they tell me, once done ten foot that was showed to be true usin a tape measure, but that's a-fore his teeth fell out. Papaw says a feller loses distance with ever' tooth that draps."

Ray-Ban could not stop grinning. "What about yo' granny?"

Not picking up on the joke, Skeeter said, "Proper ladies dont chaw 'cause the spittin and all ain't polite. She be dead now, but Mamaw dipped snuff and smoked her pipe."

Ray-Ban howled and slapped his thigh. "Gawd-*damn*! he said.

◊ ◊ ◊

"I was let out'n the mines when a roof timber fell and busted a knuckle in my backbone. Hit still pains me grievous after all these years. The hurt goes clear through my buttbone and down this one leg. That's how come I walk on a cane and take a reg'lar drap of mountain dew. Best hurt-killer God invented. Which reminds me of a story. Did I tell you young'uns 'bout Devil Anse and the revenuers? No? Well, ever'body git comfy. Skeeter, you toss another back-log on the fahr, and Jeeter, you fetch a forestick. I believe we got us enough coals banked up so's the middle dont need attendin to. The light's damn near too dim to whittle, and I wouldn't want to whittle on the end of my thumb 'stead of this here whittlin stick, would I?

"Nossir."

"Good, y'all reach them logs onto the fahr and we kin git a-goin." Papaw paused to take a sip from his jug.

"Hit was the year eighteen hunnert and eighty-nine. Charleston, hit's some seventy-five mile north. That ain't far today, but back then they warn't no roads, nor leastways roads as we'd call 'em now. Many's the time folks had to drive they wagons in the crickbeds 'cause the woods was so thick and stumpy. Well, on the night of November the nineteenth the whole city was a-buzzin. Word had went 'round that Devil Anse Hatfield, my pa, and some of his feller feudists, the ones allus battling the McCoys over to Kentucky, was seen, and they was armed. Not many believed hit, but they was another rumor that some folks looked in the winder of U.S. Deppity Marshall H. S. White's office, and shore 'nough inside set Deppity White and Devil Anse laughin and jawin peaceable as a couple of ladies at a quiltin bee. Ever'one was astounded to hyur this.

"Fer years the fed'ral gov'ment had been tryin to git Pa to Charleston to stand a-fore the law on charges of moonshinin and not payin taxes on his homemade likker. He never went, a-course, fer fear of bein arrested, and the gov'ment agents was jist as skeered of tryin to pry Pa out'n Logan County, whar he had lots of friends and relatives. But Deppity White and him was old pals, and this time he'd came down to our place and axed as a personal favor would Pa go to Charleston and put the matter to rest once and fer all. If he done hit the feds promised him protection agin the state authorities fer the constant warrants wantin his arrest in Kentucky over feudin and shootin folks." Papaw twisted in his chair and looked down at them. "I know they's two of y'all settin thar, but damned iff'n I caint see but one. Brightness of the fahr makes my nystagmus worse, that's all."

"Is this whatever you call hit worser in the daytime, Papaw?"

"Iff'n the light is bright. But the fahrlight dont make hit no picnic neither. Any brightness gives me a helluva headache. Hit's why I wear sunglasses when restin out on my settin porch in the daytime."

"Is that why your eyes go all fluttery and roll 'round like pinballs?"

"Yup. Anyhow, the two of em—that'd be my pa Devil Anse and Deppity White—set a-front our big fahrplace that night jawin and sippin Pa's homemade white likker while the cold wind was whistlin outside, sorta like tonight. Pa tuk to scratchin his whiskers, which he done when thinkin heavy thoughts, and when they turned in Pa give Deppity White the best bed, as he allus done with comp'ny. The next mornin after a breakfast of acorn coffee, ham, and hoecakes, Pa said he'd do hit and off'n they went to catch the train out'n Logan Town, Pa a-toten his Sunday suit, which they say was blue.

"In court Pa swore on a Bible to tell the truth, even though he dint believe nothin inside of hit. The judge axed Pa iff'n he was the Anderson Hatfield borned the nineth of September eighteen hunnert and thirty-eight who had married Levicy Chafin, and was he the son of Ephraim Hatfield who went by the name of 'Big Eaf,' and he agreed he was. I kin tell y'all what Pa said to that court about makin likker, more or less. Folks who was present turned his words into kind of like a poem, and later two young fellers with a banjo and a dulcimer even made a song out'n 'em. Jist about ever'body learnt the words, even young-uns like y'all. Now, go on and tap your feet with mine while I say 'em. Ready?

This corn is mine.
I seeded and weeded hit,
growed and hoed hit,

plucked and shucked hit,
and toted hit to the shuck pen.
I pounded and grounded hit,
put ever'thin into hit,
usin the plow,
and the sweat of my brow.
Iff'n I eat hit or drink hit,
give hit away or sell hit,
ain't nobody's goddamn bidness but my own,
includin the gov'ment's.
But if the truth be told,
I ain't never sold,
no man a drap of my likker,
and y'all ain't got proof that I did.

"Now, you set them words to music and it makes for a sprightly tune. Pa was right, and hit tuk the jury only a few minutes to find him not guilty of all charges. Then Pa had to sign a paper. He looked at the lawyer feller the court had give over to him that day so Pa dint say nothin illegal agin hisself. The feller nodded, and Pa made his mark where they said to. Ever'body in the courtroom cheered, and the judge declared that no state officer was to touch Pa. He directed Deppity White and some of his fed'ral men to see that Pa was put on the train back to Logan Town unharmed. As they was a-goin out the door the judge hollered, 'Feel free to arrest Mr. Hatfield when he gits home, iff'n y'all wants to try!' That's when the crowd inside and outside both got 'em a good belly-laugh."

◊ ◊ ◊

Journal entry Skeeter recently repeated to me a story his papaw had told him when he was a child. It was about his great-grandfather "Devil Anse" Hatfield and how he outsmarted the federal revenuers keen on jailing him for illegally selling moonshine and not paying taxes on it, and the state authorities for trying to extradite him to Kentucky to face charges there. A fine tale, to be sure, and it segues directly into how I hope someday to blend certain aspects neuroscience and quantum physics and explain them with every-day examples. One of these common areas might be superposition, a state fundamental to the quantum world and a concept that apt analogies would make its comprehension easier. Basically, it holds that quantum states of particles like photons and electrons can be additive to form another quantum state; on the flip side, every quantum state can be seen as the sum of two other distinct states. Put differently, between an electron's appearance at one location and its subsequent position at another it has no exact position, only the probability of where it will next appear, as I described in an earlier posting. At such times, the electron is said to exist in *superposition.*

Aspects of Skeeter's story reminded me immediately of Erwin Schrödinger's famous thought experiment of 1935 illustrating the paradox of a cat simultaneously alive and dead—in superposition, in other words. Schrödinger described his hypothetical experiment as follows. A cat is locked inside a "diabolical device" consisting of a steel box containing a Geiger counter, a glass flask of hydrocyanic acid set underneath a hammer, and a radioactive compound in a quantity so minute that over the course of an hour perhaps only a single atom decays. Radioactivity is a quantum phenomenon, and no decay is equally probable. If within this predetermined period of time (one hour) the compound decays and releases a radioactive particle the Geiger counter activates a relay, tripping the hammer. The vial is smashed, freeing the cyanide, and the cat dies. If decay is delayed at least until past the hour then the Geiger counter detects no radioactivity. Nothing further happens, and the cat survives. By one interpretation, during this critical interval of waiting the cat is poised in superposition, simultaneously alive and dead (or, you could say, neither alive nor dead). Not until the deadline passes and the box is opened can its actual status be ascertained. Opening the box constitutes an observation (i.e. a measurement), and instantaneously the wave function that has sustained the state of abeyance manifested as superposition collapses. In the quantum world, observation affects the outcome.

When the rumor circulated of "Devil Anse" Hatfield being in Charleston that November night of 1889 we can surmise he might have been in either of two places, there in Charleston or at home in Logan County. Could he have been in both places at once? Had he been a quantum the answer might be yes, provided he was in superposition. However, someone looking through the window of Deputy Marshall H. S. White's office and seeing him was the equivalent moment of opening Schrödinger's metal box and observing the cat. Sure enough, "Devil Anse" was in Charleston, although only when someone actually observed him did the wave function collapse into one of the two possible states, Charleston or Logan County.

Bivouac in the rainforest. Darkness descending, and too few photons striking the page for me to see what I write. Time to close this posting, future reader. The quantum voices in my head are superpositioned; their future status, by definition, eludes me.

◊ ◊ ◊

Journal entry Skeeter is opening up to me a little more each day, and I have learned not to expect too much in the way of self-reflection. The landscape of his musings presents a bleak geography. I picture it as a monotonous desert stretching to the horizon, sterile and monochromatic, its vista unmarred by intellectual relief. The possibility of hills and valleys seems non-existent. There are no challenging chasms to cross, circuitous paths to navigate, nothing from his perspective worth stopping to inspect. There is no life, only sterility. In that place unstirred by the breezes of curiosity Skeeter's mental world is insulated from its own interiority. His *tabula rasa* status stays intact. His sense of self no longer exists, and doubtfully ever did. Heautoscopy, like a monstrous epiboly, has smothered it.

◊ ◊ ◊

"Now, which of y'all be the oldest? I tend to fergit my rememberin sometimes."

"I'm Jeeter, and I'm the oldest. I'm a-goin on nine right soon, and Skeeter's jist eight."

"I thought y'all was twins."

"Almost."

"Who was hit said that?"

"Jeeter agin. That's me."

"Why dont Skeeter speak up?"

"'Cause he's a peckerwood, Papaw."

"Don't talk thataway, son. Y'all's brothers. He's your'n and you be his'n, so they's a need fer one another. Be glad you ain't sent underground to a breaker shed like I was at eight year old, or tharabouts. We was hunched all day over a conveyer pickin the slate from the coal and tossin hit aside, and if a boy screwed up they was a foreman with a switch.

"I had three sons. One's Everett, your pa, the other'uns is y'all's uncles Millard and Willard, who was twins. I dont recollect which be the oldest, but Millard, I think hit was. Then the youngest twin up and died. That would've been Willard, I believe, and Millard ain't been right in the head since. He was about the same age as y'all is today, Willard was, when he up and died. That was a sad time. They was like two peas in a pod. Your mamaw could tell 'em apart easy, but not me, so I got 'em to leavin the fernint straps of they overalls hangin loose. Millard's was the right one and Willard's the left." He paused and took a sip from the jug. "Or mebbe hit was the other way 'round." He scratched the back of his neck. "Hit's the funniest thang, but I jist caint recall which was which.

"I do recall that my mama, the former Levicy Chafin, dint have no teeth a-tall even way back when I was a leetle shaver. In summer she set out on the porch swing with a bowl of fresh-picked snapbeans in her lap and a empty bowl beside of her, and she'd ready snapbeans on hot afternoons. She'd send the older girls out'n the woods and fields with tow sacks to gather up pokeweed for salads and ramps to flavor the taters and turnips. They was allus chickens at her feet or scratchin in the yard close by, and she throwed the ends of them beans to 'em as she broke 'em off. Then she tuk a unsnapped bean from the bowl in her lap, snapped the ends off'n hit, and put the finished bean in the other bowl beside of her. We was a big family, and she snapped a heap of beans to make one supper. She allus had on a print dress, and she wore a man's felt hat on her head and a man's boots on her feet, and iff'n she warn't puffin on her long-stem pipe she was dippin snuff. Yup, that was Mama alright. She never said much, and both her and Pa let us young-uns run wild. They never yelled at us nor spanked us. Mebbe hit's why most of us turned up on'ry, 'specially my older brother Cap. He was a mean, wall-eyed sumbitch. Now, whar was I? Oh, yeah. What I been sayin is hit ain't the Hatfield way to be mean to close kin, so be kind to one another, hyur me?"

"Yessir, we hyur you, Papaw."

"Good. Let's git that fahr built up so's we kin tell some stories and I kin git to my whittlin, which I'm woeful behind on. Got this hyur new stick with nary a notch in hit."

"Papaw, what's a 'shaver?'"

"Lemme ponder a tad. Take this hyur whittlin stick. Pretend I'm the stick, and when I cut out a piece of wood from hit think of hit as a shavin, a wood shavin. Now, I got three sons, and they be the shavers, pieces of me, git hit?

"Yup."

"Then why ain't y'all a-buildin on that fahr yonder? Hop to hit or we liable to be hyur all night."

◊ ◊ ◊

Journal entry I notice from viewing earlier postings that I have largely neglected a critical aspect of neurological/psychological studies, the co-called "self": what it is, where it resides, and why we need it. I qualify the term with quotation marks in this posting for reasons to be explained. Certainly, a disrupted sense of himself—maybe I should reword this sentence to state that a disrupted sense of his "self"—is the basis of Skeeter's heautoscopic hallucinations, as it is in many mental diseases. I need to jot down these few thoughts to clarify the association again in my own mind. To start with, to have a "self" is to have the "phenomenal experience," or sensation, of owning it. Your "self" belongs just to you and holds the contents of consciousness; in other words, what it *feels like* to retain such ownership.

We assume that we live "inside" our bodies and there our "self" also resides. Look hard. In every brain I have dissected, nowhere among the eighty-six billion neurons and equally vast number of non-neuronal cells composing the white and gray matter did I ever come across a "self." Skeptics might claim that it could have been there all along, cryptic and disguised, and I simply did not recognize it. Fair enough, although all evidence points in another direction. So, where does the "self" reside? The answer? Nowhere. There are no such entities as "selves." They do not exist. What we experience is only the phenomenal experience of consciousness. Once again, that sensation of *being you*. The "self" is therefore a construct of the mind, an illusion, although a necessary one. Without "selves" we have no agency.

Underlying all mental activities is the conscious experience of being a "self." The perspective from the viewpoint of the "self," or of you looking out from it, is just that. Indeed, "first person singular," "I," and "ego" are synonyms, all reinforcing the notion of *being someone*. A sense of "self" (call this "selfhood") is transparent, so integral that the mind sees through it unaware of the mechanisms generating our thoughts and feelings, those physical activities happening in the brain, the biochemical shifts and flowing electrical impulses. In other words, we are unaware of how the sausage is being manufactured inside our heads. We are aware only of the *representations* the brain generates. This *phenomenal transparency* renders the object viewed, say, the color blue, inaccessible to subjective experience (i.e. to the process). Like breathing and other autonomic functions the illusion of the "self" is present in the moment and always has been, ticking away in the background, constantly performing its ghostly task of maintaining that sense of your*self*.

◊ ◊ ◊

Journal entry The world we perceive is not real. It is a simulacrum, an illusion appearing as a phenomenally transparent representation. These illusions are "transparent" to us because we are unable to recognize them *as* representations and believe we are interacting with the world directly. To use an analogy, you are looking into an aquarium when a fish swims past. You see the fish, not the aquarium glass. This is the structure of our perspectival world: transparent windows inaccessible to conscious awareness; that is, to introspection through the "mind's eye." Other properties are opaque: they register in consciousness, and we are aware of them. When we observe a cloudless blue sky we experience the *sensation* of blueness, which is transparent and unavailable for introspection. Color vision allows us to *see* the blue because it is opaque; in other words, its *content property* is blue.

I emphasize that "conscious awareness" is not tautologous. Minimal consciousness is simply the "appearance" of the world through one or more sensory mechanisms. A fish has this capability, and so does a grasshopper. Call it "awareness" of surroundings and the capacity to interpret signals from the environment. However, if we include in this definition the capacity to detect and react to chemical phenomena then no organisms can be excluded, not even microbes and plants. Obviously, "awareness" does not necessarily imply consciousness.

Our limitations are those of our senses and the brain's facility to interpret the signals they relay. The rapidity of the process renders the brain invisible to itself. Consequently, we experience just phenomenal content; representations, in other words, while never seeing them *as* representations but instead as uniquely human manifestations of reality. The result is the illusion of being in direct contact with the world when what we perceive is merely the world *as we experience it.* As naïve realists navigating through an illusion, we take for granted its reality. And the simulacrums we experience have the severe limitations of a human perspective. There are myriad competing descriptors of "reality," themselves representations. We are not alone on Earth. Reality in whatever guise is not exclusively ours. As N. Kathryn Hayles wrote, "If every species constructs for itself a different world, which is the world?"

◊ ◊ ◊

Journal entry During a heautoscopic hallucination the feeling of selfhood turns opaque, the comfort of unconscious transparency is temporarily lost, and the self disintegrates for as long as the hallucination lasts.

What the sufferer of autoscopy longs for is complete union, not separation, but that prospect is terrifying because it could mean the termination of the self if it is absorbed by the Other. In the subject's mind, the Other is out to subsume or even kill his subjectivity. In such a vulnerable state his ontological status has weakened and become a festering lesion, a site open to attack now visible to the Other and also to himself. The significance of a heautoscopic experience is the psychological affinity the subject feels for his *doppelgänger,* and the strength of his depersonalization correlates negatively to his hallucination's personalization, sometimes to the extent that the localization of the real self becomes ambiguous. In quantum-speak, the onset of an autoscopic experience marks disintegration of the psyche's normal status, which strives to retain all components of the self in rigid superposition. The three dimensions of selfhood—self-identification, self-localization, first-person perception—crumble during a heautoscopic episode (notably so if the first-person perception is weak), sometimes confusing the distinction between the hallucination and the physical body.

This state can be heightened by the preserved lateral asymmetries—absence of mirror-reversal and retention of "sidedness"—giving added realism to the projection. As the experience switches between ego – and alter ego-centered perspectives the psychological interactions between the subject and the *doppelgänger* become more unstable and unpredictable, especially if the alter ego gains autonomy, perhaps humiliating the subject and berating him. He can then lose control.

The ego lives alone in a narrow tunnel. Perhaps more accurately, *we are* the tunnels our egos inhabit. Paradoxically, this confinement leads to a false sense of freedom from the tunnel's imprisoning walls. We call it free-will. Our separate ego tunnels are packed together like the individual cells of bees and other eusocial insects in humanity's great community hive. Not surprisingly, no one actually understands or listens to anyone else. We talk past each other because sound is ephemeral. Those words we should remember, we forget; others we should forget we remember as mindless slogans to use against conspecifics, defined as those occupying different tunnels who constitute the Other. Language, when reduced to its applications and consequences, is no less primitive than the vocal signals of our fellow primates. We might as well be signaling visually in the manner of chacma baboons, using our asses and noses. These features of baboon anatomy are colorful and the messages clear.

Under normal conditions the walls of our ego tunnels are so perfectly transparent that we see through them to our illusion of the world, unaware of their existence. Even the brain is fooled, believing that what it perceives and interprets actually *is* the real world and not a simulacrum. A heautoscopic hallucination cripples the ego, immobilizing it. Then the walls of its ego tunnel turn opaque. With loss of transparency the first-person perspective weakens, identification of the self and sense of place fade, and selfhood dissolves.

There is no escaping our ego tunnels except through death. Our contact with others occurs only during delusional moments when we falsely believe our minds are merging with those sequestering in their own tunnels. We are born alone and die that way. At birth, our personal tunnel becomes manifested; at death it collapses like a quantum wave, never to form again and reappear.

◊ ◊ ◊

He finally came to rest face-down on the smoldering earth from which everything green had been vaporized, dimly aware of low flames rising from his body, of his skin newly peeled away, of his ears popping from the abrupt pressure differential. The supersonic shock wave of static pressure generated by the mortar had raced across him faster than the speed of sound, lifting then pounding him against the earth with tremendous punch. In the retreating blast-wind, shrapnel and rock fragments battered him as they sought to fill the vacuum where the ordnance had landed. He too was dragged back toward the source of the explosion, tossed and rolling, helpless as a rag-doll in a hurricane. The remaining air in his lungs departed momentarily in the vacuum's fierce embrace. In excruciating pain he screamed but sensed no sound emerge. With his lungs deflated maybe there was none and he only imagined it. The wind's passing had left his mouth stuffed with dirt. He tried to move, feeling a need to stand and run, muscles and tendons failing to acknowledge any directives, brain focused instead on unrealized damage assessment, trying to reassemble and reboot its traumatized neurons. His limbs—in fact, his entire corporeal being—had become deafferented and incapable of proprioception. He willed his muscles to move but nothing happened, and he lay as the retreating blast-wind had left him, contorted as a fallen marionette and completely still.

A lightning storm crashed against his eyes; in his ears a thousand cicadas vibrated their tymbals in unison. Visual snippets from a hellish slideshow appeared randomly and vanished in nanoseconds: faces, objects without context, vistas, headlights in fog. . . .There was no pattern, no underlying logic to what the brain had selected to *re*-present from its archive of episodic memories. Then the familiar voice in his head, this time with a different message. Jeeter was pleading with him to get up and run or they would both die. It was the first time he had heard Jeeter speak in desperation instead of the usual sarcasm and taunts. Jeeter was afraid, and knowing this offered a momentary joy.

Had Anax been watching he might have described this situation differently: he fell and did not get up, held there by entropy. The mechanical energy released when he hit the ground was transferred into heat according to the second law of thermodynamics; otherwise, his body never could have come to rest, and he would rebound forever. But Anax and the team were not watching, nor would they ever get up. They were dead.

◊ ◊ ◊

A corpsman shouted in his ear, the words barely audible against the blended cacophony of bombardment and the intense tinnitus inside his ears. He turned his head slowly and opened one eye, perceiving only dim light and the unresolved image of a man's face. The world seemed slow, dreamlike, derealized. He was lifted onto a litter and jounced roughly to an idling medivac, feeling the rushing downdraft from the spinning rotors, sensing more than hearing the revving engine, then a fleeting weightlessness at liftoff. Once aloft the world became disorienting and deafening, the starboard door gunner contributing as he strafed the ground below.

"I caint see. I got the nystagmus."

The corpsman crept forward. "You got *what?* Never heard of it. Flash blindness, probably. You were looking toward the mortar when it hit. The flash bleached your retinal pigment, but it'll reform. You're also concussed. Never mind that, Marine. You've got a shitload of worse problems. Try not to die on me, okay? The rest of your team is toast." He nodded toward the piled body bags.

For the first time he had the inchoate experience of remembering snatches of Anax's ramblings that he assumed never had been stored in memory. Suddenly, entire sentences returned giving an illusion of having participated in a dialogue. As his brain sought to rewire itself he screamed intermittently, a sound barely noticeable above the ambient noise. From the stretcher he watched through the port door as a murmuration of small birds darted and shifted in unison, flying wingtip to wingtip without touching, diving and dipping, turning abruptly, each individual aligning itself with the rest as neither a leader nor a follower. They stopped suddenly, frozen in that configuration as in a photograph, and he perceived the exact distances separating the ends of their flight feathers, heard the whirr of insubstantial vortices, felt the hesitant drag on the air. For an instant he was among them. In that brief interval he felt alone for the first time, and it was exhilarating.

The morphine should have zoned him out, but instead of dozing he was fully awake. His surroundings appeared in glittering clarity as if everything formerly invisible beneath the surface of consciousness had awakened and gained form and presence. He saw each object's essential nature. The floor of the aircraft writhed and twisted like a silvery reptile imprisoned by rivets. He believed he could see stones far below baking in the heat and inhaled the mineral smell of their molecular latices. He remembered the coffee can filled with bacon grease for frying that Mama kept on the windowsill above the sink, and the window itself, its transparency occluded by rain-streaked coal dust. He was clutching something and rubbed his thumb over its surface. Anax's journal. It must have ended up underneath him, and somehow he mustered enough kinesthetic awareness to clutch it and hold on.

The pain had spiked to a level of exquisite holiness, and he welcomed it as might an ascetic or a saint. How strange that rapture should exist in such a torched meadow of sorrow. When he screamed it was in bliss. He felt indescribable sensations, intuitively recognizing the surge of accelerating millenniums; he entered the interiors of mountains and dissolved among swarming electrons, watching transfixed as their heat-jangled Brownian movements twisted and gyrated. Then he was deep inside a different mountain surrounded by glittering coal, feeling the immense press of the Carboniferous. His lifetime experience had been that of awakening from a nightmare unsure if indeed he was awake, and if he was, why did the night persist, darkening his days?

The doc crept forward again holding another syrette, but was waved away. As he passed the crew chief he shook his head in disbelief saying, "Still conscious and turns down a second syrette. That's one tough motherfucker." Through radio static he heard the flight commander's staccato, jargon-filled report to base: heading home; five KIA in glad bags; one conscious MFW, crispy, needing triage. Rest of platoon, status unknown. Contact other dustoff, over and out. And nearly always that oddly oedipal epithet "motherfucker," the field Marine's favorite word. Call it a grammatical utility tool, adapting easily to four of the eight parts of English speech: noun, verb, adjective, and interjection.

◊ ◊ ◊

He dreamed morphine dreams, but otherwise his body cruised on autopilot, the autonomic systems continuing to motor along as they do even during consciousness. Blood pumping, air filling and exiting the lungs, neurons active but idling, processes Paul Bowles termed "the meaningless hegemony of the involuntary." It is this tyranny of the autonomic systems that dismisses rational consciousness as unnecessary and lurches blindly toward the casual detachment of death. Images appeared to him in rich color, wispy and unfocused, whirling unpredictable spirals like cigarette smoke rising lazily against the light. Sometimes there was sound unconnected to the images: gunfire and artillery explosions preceding a fleeting interregnum of silence and then the whap-whap-whap of helicopters; Scalded Creek in spring flood; undecipherable childish noises from the playground meant to elude and exclude him; the clank of coal trains wobbling slowly past, whistles insistent and bold. And sometimes strange laughter never heard before as Anax invaded his subconscious.

◊ ◊ ◊

After receiving minimal stabilization at base he was airlifted to Saigon and a month later to the big VA hospital in San Diego. From his record they found a home address, but a phone number was not included. The phone directories of southern West Virginia were replete with Hatfields. Several long-distance calls made at random failed to locate anyone related to a Hatfield having the given name of Skeeter.

Throughout these moves he had insisted that Anax's journal, which he called "my book," be near him, a request honored except during surgeries and rehabilitation sessions. Even during medevac when extraneous objects are impediments to emergency treatment he refused to relinquish it. He gripped it with such tenacity that among the numerous initial entries in his medical chart was a note about possible clenched fist syndrome. This would have been an unlikely result of the explosion and noticeably debilitating prior to it for an otherwise healthy Marine. The surgeons suspected a misdiagnosis, which proved correct.

For thirteen months he lodged at the VA hospital in San Diego undergoing what seemed to him endless surgeries, including dozens of skin grafts. Miraculously, his face, having been pressed to the ground in the aftermath of the explosion, was spared the flames except for damage to one exposed ear. He was concussed. The bones of his right leg had shattered and required several operations. The left leg was mangled too. The knee had snapped, tearing the ligaments and displacing the patella to the side, but despite all this the leg was in better shape than the right one. His pelvis had been crushed, both shoulders wrenched from the sockets. Several ribs and the right collarbone were broken. The many small bones of both feet had been broken and redistributed. According to a nurse his heavy boots had provided support and containment during the explosion's aftermath. Those x-rays of his feet, as he put it, looked like a game of pickup-sticks. Plan on having foot problems for life, he added helpfully. The litany went on. When at last he could stand for brief periods the painful rehabilitation sessions began, what the patients jokingly called R & R, except now the letters represented Recovery and Rehabilitation, not beers and barbecues on the beach.

◊ ◊ ◊

Pain reminds us we are alive, a prod to the self never to relax into a state in which only consciousness exists. Pain refutes Descartes' notion of dualism. It lets the mind know that it and the body are inseparable. You might describe your pain to others, but it can be felt only by you, and you are incapable of feeling anyone else's. As Wittgenstein said, "I can only believe that someone else is in pain, but I know it if I am." The border separating the two of you is untraversable. But in just this way pain reinforces agency and selfhood, the inherent belief in your uniqueness, a reminder of your existence and proof you are alive because the pain is *yours*. The right dorsal anterior cingulate cortex responds to our own pain and also when we see someone else in pain. However, the primary somatosensory cortex shows only a sensory response (the actual pain) in both instances, but not the visual (emotional) response. Therefore, to tell someone else you "feel his pain" means that you are sensitive to his emotional state while insensate to the hurt.

Fever dreams as his immune system beat back raging infections; morphine clouds lifting intermittently admit anomia that clung like a recalcitrant meniscus to the sagging walls of memory. He drifted in and out of consciousness experiencing a great interior silence accompanied by a feeling of persistent calm. Although never introspective, in this new state he realized in a burgeoning clairvoyance that attention to the self was not required, and he became aware of a spreading stillness that seeped into his pores and from there to his circulatory system until he felt immersed in a vast plasma that made him one with the cosmos, and he intuitively understood what Anax had meant when he said that we are made of stardust. The feeling had subsumed him, this empty awareness dissociated from ego and intellect; he became that person each of us actually is but admits reluctantly. He had become no one and paradoxically felt reassured.

He was reminded of something else Anax said, hearing it dutifully and understanding not a word. It was that we need the illusion of a self to interpret our place in the world, which is directed by perceptions, but that during periods of anoesis our perceptions vanish leaving us without a window on the world. In their place is the experience of feeling nothingness, the complete absence of the self.

◊ ◊ ◊

At his exit interview he was instructed to provide a mailing address for the disability checks. He told the clerk to send them in his name to the company store, Scalded Creek, West Virginia. The clerk asked if there was a street name or post office box. "Nope," he said. "We only got but one street. Hit dont have a name and hit ain't much of a street, mostly mud in winter and dust in summer. Them checks, they'll find me alright."

He was given plane tickets from San Diego through Chicago and Pittsburgh to Charleston. From there, he was to take a taxi to the bus station and buy a ticket to ride the last seventy-five miles south down state route 10 through Logan and Man to Scalded Creek.

He arrived at the bus station exhausted and in considerable pain from standing and walking, conditions worsened by the stress of navigating through airports in cities where he had never been, and from lack of sleep. The driver tossed his duffel into the luggage compartment before looking at him, and when he did, he said, "What the hell happened to you, boy? Car wreck?"

The questions startled him. He could not think of a suitable reply and said simply, "Viet Cong."

The driver slammed the compartment door shut and turned the handle. "I was in Korea myself. Army. Fuckin gooks. Whar you figger me to drap you?"

"Scalded Crick at the bridge. That'd be fine."

The driver nodded. "I know hit. Jump aboard, Marine. Shoulda noticed hit on your duffel. Mind that cane, you dont trip nobody up. In fact, set in the first seat to the left. More leg room."

◊ ◊ ◊

The bus let him off at the edge of the hard road where the one-lane bridge crossed Scalded Creek to the eponymous coal camp. The place seemed familiar, yet strange and somehow unreal. How was it possible to be back where he started? Halfway around the world and now here again. The driver graciously yanked his duffel out and carried it to the foot of the bridge, gave an informal salute, and stepped back aboard. He had been awake nearly two days with nothing to eat and drink except vending machine snacks and water from drinking fountains.

The air still stank of sulfur from the slate dump. He dragged the duffel off to the side, in case a vehicle needed to cross the bridge, and stared down at the coal-stained water flowing sluggishly past. He remembered how he and the other boys would sit on the concrete wingwall spitting tobacco juice and threatening to push one another over the edge where the drop was about eight feet. The bridge itself was not more than thirty feet across but seemed shorter now. He took in the scene and thought how everything appeared shrunken and shabby and wondered why in childhood the world was so much more expansive.

He was aware of a pickup behind him slowing to pull onto the bridge. It came even and stopped. The driver leaned over the passenger side and rolled down the window. He was wearing a patch over one eye. "That you, Skeeter?"

He looked back. "Odie? Odie Chafin? Yeah, I reckon hit's me alright."

"Back from Nam, Skeeter?"

"Yup. With a stop at a hospital in California whar

they sewed the pieces back together, more or less."

"Well, I'll be doggone. Hop on in. I'll throw your duffel in the bed."

"I'll try and climb in. I dont do much hoppin anymore."

"I see that. Take your time."

After Odie returned and slid under the steering wheel they shook hands. Odie looked different, not surprising with the passing of time. He obviously did too. Odie was heavier and his hairline was receding, and then there was that eyepatch, something else that seemed both familiar and strange.

"You home fer good?"

"Seems like hit. Dint know whar else to go. I reckon you kin drap me at the cabin, iff'n hit's still thar."

"Okey-doke, but let me run to the comp'ny store first and git us a cold sixer to sorta celebrate your homecomin."

"I feel like sleepin, but a coupla cold ones won't hurt. You got the time?"

"Yup. I'm off'n work today and jist run to Man fer some odds and ends. I tuk bookkeepin in high school, and now I'm bookkeeper over to the sawmill whar your uncle Millard worked. Shame he died."

"Uncle Millard died?"

"Yup, 'round three year ago, I believe. Heart attack. Drapped dead in front of the big ripsaw. They said he was gone a-fore hittin the sawdust. You dint know?" Skeeter shook his head.

"Wal, hyur we be at the store. Set tight. Be back dreckly." Skeeter held out a five-dollar bill, but Odie waved it away. "On me."

◊ ◊ ◊

The cabin looked about the same as before, showing few signs of desuetude. The weeds had grown up, but that was the only obvious difference from his recollection. Papaw's shed and porch, the same. They pushed open the back door of the cabin and went inside through the mudroom. No door in Scalded Creek had a lock. Everything was covered with a fine patina of coal dust. The rooms smelled of stagnant air and abandonment. "How long has this place been empty?"

Odie looked surprised. "I reckon you ain't heard a word since leavin, so I'll start back a ways. Your mama died of a head injury not long after you left. Your pa claimed she fell, but others believed he smacked her too hard or too many times. A-course they warn't no proof, so folks jist let it go as some of the shit that happens in coal camps and ain't none of nobody's bidness.

"Then your pa's black lung hit him hard, and he tuk to his bed. Your papaw saw him thar and figgered he was sleepin, but your papaw had got so he lost track of time and couldn't remember nothin. Warn't 'til a week or two later, nobody really knowed how long, when he finally told your uncle how the cabin was a-smellin bad. Millard went to check, and after the burial he let hit be knowed at the sawmill that his brother had been dead a piece of time and Papaw never noticed. A normal person, he said, would've smelt the smell a lot sooner. Your papaw, he was livin in your old room and walked back and forth past the open door to your pa's bedroom. Must've seed him layin thar but dint notice they warn't no twitch left in him. Nobody was lookin in on 'em. Don't know what they'd been eatin. Hyur, let me reach us another beer. I also got some chips and pre-made sandwiches. Holp yourself."

They sat in the living room, the place where Pa had routinely beaten the hell out of him. Odie said, "Your ma, pa, and Uncle Millard, they's buried up to the cemetery in the Hatfield section. Want to see the graves?"

"Nope. Thanks anyways, Odie, but I ain't interested in 'em. Pa was bodacious mean, and I'd as soon fergit the sumbitch. He dint do nothin but beat on me and Mama. Bein in the fuckin Marines was easier'n livin hyur." He thought momentarily how Pa must have died angry or sad, or likely both.

They sat a while in silence, then Odie said, "What you figger on a-doin? Fer work, I mean."

"Cain't do much. All crippled up like this I ain't even fit fer found work. Reckon I'll live on the disability pension the gov'ment give me. It ain't much, but I dont need a whole lot."

They found the ignition key to Pa's truck in a kitchen drawer and went outside. The battery was dead, as expected. "How long's hit been settin? Prob'ly Uncle Millard used hit some."

"He did. I'd see hit parked up to the sawmill on occasion, but caint say how long hit's been settin hyur." They tried jumping it using Odie's truck, to no avail.

"Iff'n you kin wait 'til Sunday when I'm off we kin fahr hit up then. I'll run into Man on Saturday after work and git a new battery."

"How much you figger?" He reached for his wallet, but Odie waved his hand.

"I'll bring the receipt Sunday. You kin pay me then. Got food to last a coupla days?"

"Prob'ly. Must be some canned goods in the pantry. And thanks fer the holp, Odie."

Odie stopped and turned at the door. "One more thing. Sim Copley's managin the comp'ny store these days. You was already gone when he started. Anyways, I'll stop by and ax him to turn your 'lectric on."

After Odie left he pulled the coverlet from the bed, dragged it outside, and shook it as best he could. Someone had put down clean bedclothes and made up the bed after they took away Pa's body.

He undressed, fell onto the mattress, and dreamed of Mama. She was standing alone in a wedge of shadow thrown off by the partly open kitchen door. Her shoulders were slumped, hands hanging by her sides. She was crying in intermittent little sobs, the sound strange and barely audible like the mewling of a kitten. He started to hug her until a hulking presence pulled him back and warned him not move. It seemed that Mama stood in that shadow the longest time, although in dreams a minute can seem eternity. He awoke with an inchoate recollection of her chronic fear and ination but could not recall the particulars of her face, except that it was long and sad and riven with tears.

◊ ◊ ◊

The church bell was ringing as he hobbled to the bridge and pulled himself onto one of the two concrete wingwalls that served double duty as railings. The walls were about four feet high, the edges perhaps eight inches thick. He arranged himself on one, feet dangling over the side. He looked down into the creek and hawked a stream of ambeer at its shiny black surface. "Take that," he muttered.

In the bright light of morning the surroundings were becoming comfortable. His presence of place seemed to be expanding as if in childhood. This wall had seemed higher then, the short drop to the water intimidating. There was room to become lost in every direction. A child's perspectival world is qualitative, contained within an elastic consciousness that expands and contracts like lungs, breathing in experiences and expelling them in modified configurations. Set-pieces are not quantitative: objects and spaces are not counted or measured as adults do for utility and archival purposes, but lived in terms of their immediate properties. A chair eventually becomes a seat, but not before being an object to support yourself while learning to stand, or to push around and then fall against and bang your head.

He considered that at one time he actually had the option of not returning home. It was during R & R one night on China Beach. He and Weasel had bumped into each other, neither actually drunk although well along. Guys were feeling charitable in these clean, safe surroundings, and Weasel had grabbed his arm and started talking about going home after his hitch. He apologized to Skeeter for ragging on him about his shadow and for walking away without having said anything after the tail-end Charlie incident. "I mean, shit, I'd of prob'ly did the same. After a while, a guy gets to where he can't take anymore, he's fed up. What do they call that where you come from?"

"The yips," he had said.

"Well, I been meanin to talk to you about maybe relocatin after you muster out. I think you and me could become good buddies. I'm from Flint."

"Whar's that?"

"Up in Michigan. My dad's got a job on the assembly line at General Motors makin Chevys. It's really somethin to see them things start as a pile of parts and end up brand new cars at the end of the line. It's union work and pays real good. That's where I'm headed after I'm the fuck outta the Corps. My dad's gettin me a job on the line, and he could have you put on too. Hell, Mom and Dad bought our house when Dad got him that job after he mustered out of the Navy, so workin for GM is a pretty good deal. What're your plans when we rotate back to the World and they let us go?"

"Coal mines, I reckon. Not much else to do in Logan County. Money's good thar too, and hit's union."

"Yeah, but it's dangerous. I've heard about them cave-ins and fires and such. And don't guys turn sick from the dust?"

"Yup. My pa's got black lung right now, iff'n hit ain't already kilted him."

Skeeter had wondered aloud how far this Flint was from Logan County, and Weasel answered that he had no idea, but a helluva lot closer than it is from China Beach, and they laughed. The discussion was then paused, and later the mortar attack changed everything.

Just then Odie pulled onto the bridge and stopped.

"Mornin. Went by your place and figgered you might be hyur spittin in the crick like old times. Got the battery and stopped at the store fer sandwiches and beer. Ready to git workin?"

He clambered off the wingwall and grabbed his cane. "Yup. Let's git at hit."

"Wal, hop in or crawl in, whichever hit's easier."

A new battery was the answer. Pa's truck started at once, but ran roughly. They removed the air filter and adjusted the carburetor until the idle evened out. Afterward, they sat in the shade on Papaw's settin porch and ate lunch.

"I been a-meanin to say I'm real sorry fer causin your eye troubles, Odie."

"Hit's okay, Skeeter, jist a accident 'tween kids. Coulda been anybody, but hit was me. Luck of the draw. My pa never did buy that BB gun off'n your pa. Mama said, no way."

"Does hit bother you grievous hard havin jist one eye?'

"At first, but I've got used to hit, sorta. That BB done turned the eyeball to mush. Nothin the doctors over to Logan could do. They tuk hit out and stuck a glass one in the eyehole, but the colors dint match and it dint turn in, what do they call it, synchrony with the other'n. Hit's still inside thar, but I jist wear a patch instead so's I dont look like a doofus."

"Well, I'm truly sorry and wished it dint ever happen, or happened to somebody else."

"Me too, but what the hell. And who might you wish this on?"

"Never mind, jist my mouth runnin without axin the brain first was hit a stupid thing to say. Jist some asshole I know." He changed subjects abruptly. "Hit's nice of you to holp with the truck and set with me on your day off, but what about your family?"

"Don't have one. Parents and grandparents is dead. Got a aunt over to Huntington I ain't seed since I was a kid. Never had a brother nor a sister. So hit's jist me alone in the cabin at the other end of the camp, same as you over hyur."

"I reckon we could git us some girlfriends," he said with a grin.

Odie barked a laugh and slapped his thigh. "That's a good-un. Any woman takin a gander at us is liable to run away fast as she kin on her gitaway sticks. Me bein half blind won't see whar she's run to, and you with them bum legs sure as hell ain't gonna ketch her."

◊ ◊ ◊

He dreaded that first trip to the company store with its steep flight of stairs. As a kid he had run up and down them countless times, but as a handicapped adult they seemed foreboding. At all hours of the day and night the warped boards served as makeshift bleachers for loafing miners retired or off shift, some sitting alone with smokes or chaws, others involved in murmured conversations. It was strictly a male enclave where union matters and masculine topics like the various merits of certain pickups and guns were discussed and debated. They paused and nodded acknowledgment as he struggled upward dragging his worse leg a step at a time, lifting their beers out of the way and shifting to make way for his cane. They understood, as he did, that he would be forever among them but never again of them. His service and wounds were admired, of course. No one doubted he had been in the shit. However, his pension was military, not union negotiated, the weapons he once carried designed for shooting men, not rabbits and squirrels. There could be no real commonality. But the undercurrent of Otherness flowed deeper, eliciting in them a twinge of childish guilt: a glance at his misshapen flesh layering the shattered bone brought into true perspective any ridiculous notion that testicles somehow correlate with either horsepower or the capacity to kill at a distance.

He reached the door and pushed inside. The arrangement was pretty much as he remembered. He took a cart and turned down an aisle lined with shelves of canned goods. These, along with some fresh produce and cheap cuts of meat, would be his staples. The top shelf just beyond his fingertips held an assortment of baked beans with bacon or ham. Nearby stood a three-foot stepladder. He was about to pull it nearer with his cane, then considered the risk and instead continued down the aisle. Behind him a woman said, "I kin reach you them beans, mister. I mean, iff'n you want." He heard the ladder screech across the floor and turned to see two tippy-toed legs standing on the top step. They seemed vaguely familiar. As he looked up their owner turned and exclaimed, "Wal, I do declare! Skeeter Hatfield! I heerd you was back from Vietnam." She clamored down, dumped several cans into the cart, and hugged him so spontaneously and hard that he stumbled backward sending cans on the lower shelves clattering to the floor. She clapped her hands over her face. "Oh, I'm so sorry! I dint mean. . . .Hyur, let me holp you up." She bent down, tripping over the cans and falling on top of him, striking his nose with her forehead and causing it to bleed. "Oh, my God! I've went and did hit agin," she said, struggling to stand while trying to hold down her dress. Then she grabbed his hand and yanked him upright.

"My cane," he said, marveling at her strength and energy.

She picked it up and handed it to him while he steadied himself using the cart. "Yep, you done hit agin," he said. Tears swelled her eyes. "Seems like ever' time I see Mary Robert Vance hit gits me a bloody nose." Then they started to laugh. She rummaged in a pocket of her dress for a hanky and held it under his nose to dam the flow.

◊ ◊ ◊

"I allus seed myself as hard-favored, so I caint picture a looker like you takin time to bloody somebody busted up as me."

She dabbed some blood from his upper lip. "I'll tell you true," she said, "you do lean to the hard-favored side, but a man is more'n that. You know this from other women you've tuk up with. And yeah, you surely been busted up a lot since last I seed you. I reckon you've tuk a backset from the you of four or five year ago. You was walkin on both hindlegs then. How puny might you be besides crippled legs and other wounds I can see? I bet you got a slew more scars 'neath them clothes." Then in a soft voice she said, "I need to hursh this larpin big mouth. I got no call to insult you, jist the buck-agers is all. Sorry."

He hung his head, curious that he had made someone nervous, repressing the urge to be truthful in return and admit there never was a woman of his own, what you could call a girlfriend, only abrupt encounters with Vietnamese chippies and daydreams abbreviated to repress Jeeter's mirth and minimize his sarcastic comments.

He felt playful, overcome by a sudden internal lightness as if gravity had been suspended or an unwanted quiddity had been lifted from him. "Yeah, I got women all over the world. They love me even more since I got bollixed in the war, though I ain't near the shindigger I used to be, nor nary as handsome." He said this without forethought while leaning on his cane and grinning stupidly. Never in his life had he spoken so freely, even to Anax.

She bent forward in a gesture of examining him closely. "Oh, I dont know," she said, stepping back. "You ain't exactly sniptious, hat all lopper-jawed, a-wearin them wore out clothes hyped-up in the back, and limpin hooly on a cane. I seed a uglier face once, but hit was a road-kilt possum a-wearin hit."

"Reckon y'all better git your eyesight checked," he said. "Don't want my time beat by no dead possum." They started to laugh again, cautiously at first, then escalating quickly into hooting and sucking air to breathe. When at last it ended and they were left gasping he was aware they were looking directly into each other's eyes, and the irises of hers were light brown with limbal rings and tiny golden flecks. He had never seen anything so beautiful or recalled being so relaxed and happy. She said, "Hyur, let me pack them groceries home fer you and put 'em up. I'll finish fillin your cart with what I figger you need. Wait fer me at the checkout counter. After payin go on and git your truck and I'll do the totin and loadin. I was prin near off work anyways, so you kin carry me back later to pick up my car."

◊ ◊ ◊

After loading in the groceries she hopped onto the seat beside him. "Damn!" she said. "This truck is stick shift. Kin you drive hit with them legs all broke up?"

"Barely."

She jumped out and came around to the driver's side. "Scoot over. You livin in your parents' cabin down by the crick?" He nodded. "I know whar that's at. Hyur we go. One thing we gotta do quick is dump this hyur truck. Your pa's, right?" He nodded. "Wal, hit's old and a stick and smokes terrible from needin a valve job." She glanced sideways. "Got any money?"

"A few hunnert saved, and my monthly disability pension from the gov'ment."

"That's more'n most have. What you thinkin at?"

He looked askance at her bare right leg alternately controlling the accelerator and brake pedals, the left expertly working the clutch. "I could go for a '53 Ford 239 Flathead V8 that ain't too ganted. I caint afford to hire out fer fixin one that needs a heap of work. That model's paired with a Fordomatic tranny and dont require no shiftin. I worked on one in high school mechanics shop and know hits workins 'nough to keep hit runnin on junkyard parts. At one time I thought of openin my own garage, but that was a-fore the Marines. I caint see myself layin on my back and slidin 'round on a undercar roller. Hell, I kin barely fall out'n the bed of a mornin. But I could still raise the hood and do some easy stuff without no help to save on money. Pa left a passel of tools and minded 'em good, and I'll do the same with 'em." He looked out the side window. "Iff'n I got a weakness to make a mechanic hit ain't bein as likely with the 'lectrical side as I ought'n, but seein as how stuff turned out I surely got time to study up on hit. From now on I got nothin 'cept time. I warn't much curious-turned at school, but now I wouldn't mind studyin some."

"Then we'll start a-huntin for a—what's hit agin—a '53 Ford. . . .C'mon, tell me the rest." She made a come-on gesture with her hand, playful and impatient, and he recognized in its symbolism and gamine charm and his immediate response a pleasant sensation of entrapment.

"A Ford F100 half-ton pickup, 239 Flathead V8." He liked that she had inserted herself in the upcoming hunt. They looked sideways at each other and laughed.

◊ ◊ ◊

The groceries having been put away, Mary Robert rested her hands on her hips and gazed around. "Goodness, child, dont you never red up? Hope you dint lay off buyin a broom on one of them trips to the store. Whar's hit at?"

"Used to be one in the closet yonder. The pan too."

"Well, I'll fetch 'em and give the place a sweep." She pointed to the worse of his crippled legs and chuckled "You sure as hell ain't gonna do hit, seein as how you're flyin on one wing." She looked around again. "Ha! Might need me a shovel too."

After giving his cabin a thorough sweeping she made coffee and further startled him by saying, "Iff'n you was to come a-courtin I'd not mitten you."

She seemed to be taking over his life with an unusual confidence and vigor. He was torn between feeling pleased by the attention and intimidated by her boldness. Already, Jeeter the casuist was whispering that she could not be trusted and was just after someone to pay her bills. "A woman like her takin a shine to a ugly cripple such as yourself? Don't be stupid. Get her the hell outta hyur. She wants that disability pension."

"You're dead wrong!" he said unwittingly.

Mary Robert set down her cup. "What?"

He quickly collected his wits. "Not you. I was jist talking to my legs."

She looked dubious. "Dint sound like no conversation with legs. You feelin puny, honey?"

"Tuckered is all. Ever' leetle thing wearies a body when you caint git goin without pain. Sorry. I jist dont wanna glom it up with you."

She reached across the table and patted his hand. "You ain't. I know you're dauncy. I promise not to be deef to that pain. Jist say whatever you want whenever. And dont be a-feared I'm lookin fer someone to pay my due-bills, 'cause I ain't. I got me a job at the comp'ny store holpin the customers, as you seed up close, and sometimes checkin 'em out. I dont give all of 'em a bloody nose, a-course, only the ones I like." They laughed, and she continued: "I pay rent to Mama and Pa fer my room and board and do jist fine, thank you. Now, you set a spell, and I'll fetch us some more coffee. I added yeast and wheat flour to your cart a-fore checkout, which you dint notice. I'll make some light-bread and heat up a can of beans and ham fer your supper. Won't take long." She stood and looked over her shoulder at him and smiled.

Later she told him, "Don't be a-tryin to cut a wide swath in your condition. I kin do my part and your'n besides. Some says I ain't yet married 'cause I'm funny-turned, but once folks gits to know me they see that I ain't affectin a-tall. I'm happy with store-bought'n dresses and dont need no purties to sparkle in folks' faces. As to not bein deferrin enough 'round men and havin a forward manner, I say only what's true. Don't listen to them that flaps gossipy lips. They dont know squat."

◊ ◊ ◊

Jeeter was proved wrong. Mary Robert did not quit her job at the company store despite Skeeter not caring if she did. She argued that her salary would stretch his pension, that she got an employee discount on lots of items except food and beverages, dry goods mostly, and stretched over a year that could amount to considerable savings.

Mary Robert told Skeeter she loved him. He sat

petrified. "Shut up!" he shouted. "Shut your goddamn mouth!"

Without a flinch or even blinking, she said, "I know that ain't you talkin at me, and hit'll be alright." She reached across the table and squeezed his hand. Her hand was warm and affected with comfort, a hand that transferred strength and assurance. Her eyes held no fear, only love.

She said she loved him for just who he was, the man sitting across the table from her in that moment, in that light. He staggered to his feet and lurched out the door, letting it slam behind him. He paced the yard, making it across to the other side of the truck before throwing up. How? Why? She described him as the first truly sincere man she had known, yet his façade was a lie. Always, he had hidden the true him, projecting instead his imposter in the hope of concealing the yawning emptiness inside. How could she have drilled through the veneer and not seen what he had spent his life sequestering? How could she love an empty vessel? And then of course there was Jeeter. He was baggage no sane woman would volunteer to tote.

She was tugging his arm. He turned away. She forced his head around and looked into his eyes. "I see you, Skeeter Hatfield. You kin hide from the world, but not from me, so dont even try." Suppose Mary Robert was right, and she really could see his hidden self. Where did Jeeter fit into the picture? As his alter-ego? What if Jeeter supplanted him? Certainly, they were linked like Siamese twins for life, but which was the true him, or had they been fused all along?

They walked back to the cabin, arm in arm. "Do

you love me, Skeet?"

"I reckon so."

"You *reckon so?*" She laughed and threw her arms around his neck. "Then I reckon that'll have to do me."

◊ ◊ ◊

Mary Robert scoured the penny savers and classifieds in the *Logan Banner* for several weeks before seeing a truck that met Skeeter's specifications. A retired doctor in Omar was offering it, so they drove over one Saturday after phoning first. Mary Robert said he needed a phone and arranged for one to be installed by the telephone company, a first for the cabin. It had been several weeks since the encounter in the store, and she had moved in with her clothes, dishes, and cooking utensils to the consternation of her parents, who advised strongly against it without at least a promise of marriage.

The doctor was sitting on his front porch smoking a pipe when they arrived. "Drive right up in the yard," he shouted, then commenced a painful descent to the ground aided by a cane. When he saw Skeeter's condition he brandished his cane. "I see you got one of these too. I also see that you're busted up pretty good. Vietnam?" Skeeter nodded. "You're the ones called about my truck?" Skeeter nodded again. "You sure ain't a talker."

"He gits the yips sometimes," Mary Robert said.

"Doesn't surprise me," the doctor said. "I treated boys back from Korea years ago. The medical experts called it shellshock. Now I hear on the teevee that doctors treating the brain-damaged soldiers return-ing from Vietnam have a different name for the same thing, but damned if I recall what it is." He turned to Skeeter. "Not that I'm saying you're brain-damaged, just that this malady is common among war veterans." Skeeter was silent.

The doctor leaned on his cane with both hands. "Used to be a feller named Sim Copley who ran the company store over at Scalded Creek. Know him?"

"I do," Mary Robert said. "He's my boss."

The doctor looked at Skeeter as if expecting a reply and was not disappointed. "Him and me done traded howdies but ain't shook yet."

The doctor nodded. "Well," he said, "he once came to me with a bad bellyache, and I diagnosed an inflamed gall bladder."

"He told me that," Mary Robert said. "He told me hit was causin him grievous pain but that a doctor over to Omar cured him."

"That would be me," said the doctor. "I cut it out."

"Yup, that's what he told me. Sim said, 'Dint need the sumbitch no longer.' Sorry to cuss, but hit's what he said. Funny how a person is borned with a body made by God hisself and hit goes and does you dirt. You'd of thought God knowed better."

They went behind the house where the truck was parked at the end of a bare patch of yard. "I don't use it these days, not at eighty-five years of age. My daughter carries me around to the stores when I need something, and the rest of the time I sit on the sofa and look at the teevee. Either that or hobble out to the porch in good weather and watch the world go by, or at least the world according to Omar." They examined the truck, its finish dulled, the paint originally pale blue, patches of broken-through rust on the fenders and rocker panels. The upholstery was about as expected. Overall, not in bad condition for having been left outside through the years. The doctor leaned against it. "Got to take some pressure off this bum hip," he said. He tapped the passenger door with his cane. "It's tired and worn out, same as me. I guarantee the battery's dead. You'll need to inflate the tires some and jump-start the engine once the battery is charged, but I think she'll run. There's a little gas in the tank that's been laying a while so you probably have water in the fuel line and need to drain it. Might have to spray ether in the carburetor when you go to crank her over the first time.

"Anyhow, get the damn thing resuscitated and it should run fine. It's sure to need parts, so drop by a place that when I was your age we called a junkyard. You'll recognize it real quick by rusting carcasses of cars and trucks heaped atop one another like a quorl of mating toads in springtime. There's generally a fence as if the stuff inside had value, and it might be patrolled by a rottweiler, so look real careful before stepping out. There still must be some of these places. They stock a world of used parts and sell 'em cheap. My friends and I used to scavenge there like vultures, doing surgery as necessary to keep our own junkers breathing and ambulatory, if only slightly quicker than the corroding dead all around. We drained the synovial fluid from inside moribund transmissions, once red but turned sludgy and brown like exhausted old blood. We fed and refueled with the appropriate octane, adjusted arrhythmic carburetors like cardiac surgeons, performed fuel-pump transplants, gapped ignition points with the care of orthodontists, drained and replaced the oil with a spinal fluid having the weight of its season. Shit, I'd have been a mechanic if I hadn't gone to medical school. My price is two hundred dollars. It's fair."

Mary Robert looked at Skeeter, who nodded. "I'll write you a check," she said. "Soon's we git home we'll phone fer a wrecker. Kin probably have one here dreckly, I'd say Monday or Tuesday, and then she'll be on the road to Scalded Crick."

"I'll fetch the title and registration," the doctor said. "Key's in the ignition, spare key's in the glovebox. Can I offer you some refreshment? Iced sweet tea? A cold beer? I don't see much company, so I don't mind jawing a bit."

Mary Robert turned to Skeeter. "Well, we couldn't turn such a polite offer of a cold beer, could we, sugar."

"Then settle yourselves on the porch swing. I'll be back in a jiffy." He turned and grinned. "Maybe a little longer. I don't hop to so quick these days."

◊ ◊ ◊

It was shortly before Mary Robert moved in, and he was thinking of her upbeat personality and kindness, the unusual color of her eyes. He thought about her legs, shapely and smooth-looking standing on that stool in the company store at his eye level. He had never seen their equal, although the only public place he had been that close to a woman's legs was Saigon where girls danced on the bar tops. That was different because they were chippies, not proper American girls. He and Mary Robert had known one another practically from birth, minus those consecutive years when she purposely avoided him. One thing was strange: he had no mental picture of her except the day on the softball field when they were children. Not until that morning in the store when she offered to fetch him some cans of beans from an upper shelf.

Suddenly, the ever-present voice in his mind intruded and shattered the reverie: "Skeeter, give it up, old son. A woman like her with *you?* She dont need no loser in her life, 'specially somebody ugly, stupid, crippled, and broke 'cept fer a disability pension that ain't hardly worth spit. Why dont you jist crawl off somewheres in the mountains and die? Ain't nobody gonna miss you, that's fer sure."

He was standing beside his bed. The intrusion on this rare moment of happiness when he could think about someone else and in a kindly way was too much. He shifted instantaneously into a state of erethism, shouting, cursing, slashing the air with his cane trying to kill or maim his invisible antagonist. Around and around he spun in a clumsy pirouette. Jeeter's phantom appeared intermittently, each instance with a different look on its face, the body in a different pose: laughing silently, leering, scowling. It pointed an index finger in his face, posed in an arabesque as a show of dexterity, stepped backward with chin tilted up in confidence while casting a sly sideways glance. It was like being at the movies when the film freezes on a single image, unsticks and continues, then freezes again, on and on. The images shifted closer, invading his personal space, retreating just out of range when he swiped at them with his cane. The spinning juxtapositions confused and alarmed him. He sensed his perspectival functions disintegrating, the vestibular organs in his ears dissociating from equilibrium, and as he became ever dizzier and disoriented the images rotated faster until he fainted and fell.

◊ ◊ ◊

He came to with a fierce headache, hearing a woman's voice crooning softly. He was confused and still disoriented, thinking it could only be Mama, but that was impossible. A soft, cool cloth was pressed to his brow, and a hand was stroking his cheek. Soft fabric pressed against the other cheek, and he realized that his head was in someone's lap. He opened his eyes to see Mary Robert looking down, a concerned expression on her face. "You okay, honey? I come by to drap off a meatloaf I jist made and seed you layin on the floor. You got a nasty bump on your head."

"I fell and must've banged it on the bedpost. I'm feelin wearisome, fer certain, like a man been drug through a knothole. Glad you stopped by 'cause they's somethin that needs jawin about."

"Not now. Let's git you into bed. We kin talk later. I'm goin home to pick up a few things and comin right back to spend the night. I'll fix us a nice hot supper. You shouldn't be alone."

He dreamed again of Mama, wondering why in his

memories and dreams she never smiled or laughed. In this dream he was standing in the living room looking toward the kitchen. She stood facing him, backlit by light streaming through the kitchen window. He could see only her slim outline and had the impression she was speaking softly, although he could not be sure. He turned an ear her way hearing only a concatenation of moans and sighs seemingly uttered by an imprisoned soul. Was she begging release from perpetual torment or simply trying to explain her lot? There was no way of knowing. Her elbows straightened, and he knew her hands had dropped. He perceived, without seeing, the nervous mannerism of wiping them on her apron during moments of stress. He asked if he could look at her face, and she stepped out of the bright background illumination into the dimness of the living room. When he spoke she did not respond and seemed unaware of his presence. He wondered if he might be a ghost too, invisible to others. In the sparse light she looked wrinkled and pale, like someone drowned and resuscitated.

◊ ◊ ◊

How did he become the recipient of such kindness and altruism? Except for his mother no one had ever shown so much concern for his well-being. He was convinced it was genuine, not a sly maneuver to gain access to his pension. The monthly sum it provided was not worth the investment of Mary Robert's time. She had said she loved him; it was that straightforward and honest.

He felt good enough after resting to get up and eat supper. Afterward, Mary Robert opened a bottle of wine, and they went into the living room and sat on the couch. For him, drinking wine was a new experience. Until coming home he had drunk only beer, local moonshine, and bottled spirits, mostly bourbon. But the white wine was cold and soothing.

It was time to tell Mary Robert about Jeeter, his twin who had died, to spill the whole sordid history of how he was never alone even when no one else was present. He had done this only once before, laying it out for Anax. Jeeter's presence explained why he muttered and sometimes seemed in deep conversations with himself which, as Anax had explained, he actually was. Why, when conversing with Jeeter, any bystanders might consider him insane. He described their antagonistic relationship, which nonetheless was a bond, that as Anax had put it they were psychologically conjoined to be separated only at his death. For better or worse, Jeeter would always lurk in the background. The best he could hope for would be regaining more control of the relationship.

He described how Jeeter's image appeared to him as a ghost, a haint, always on his left, although sometimes he skulked unseen behind him. Then he sensed a presence. He understood from Anax's explanations that in neither configuration was the presence "real." However, because he could not remember life without it he referred to it simply as Jeeter, as if it really was him alive inside his head. He related how Anax had said that Jeeter presented as a heautoscopic hallucination, that during one of these episodes the self—the whole of him, inside and out—is not replicated literally. What the subject—Skeeter himself—sees is a hallucination of his body in extra-personal space; that is, outside himself at a distance. Anax used the German word *doppelgänger* to define this image of a double, which actually is not a replicated "self." When having a heautoscopic experience the subject is undecided if he is disembodied and if the self has been retained within his own body or migrated instead to the hallucination. Also, he might experience seeing the world simultaneously through both bodies, or alternately back and forth.

For Skeeter it was a lot to explain, and he bumbled through as best he could. For Mary Robert, to whom this was all new, it was still more to absorb, and she tried hard to understand. "So, this haint named Jeeter is your dead identical twin brother?"

"More or less."

"And you and this haint ain't never been apart from one another?"

"That's right."

"So, when I see you talkin to yourself, hit's really Jeeter's haint you're talkin to, and y'all is havin a conversation together?"

"That's the gist of hit. You decide iff'n I'm crazy or hainted by a dead ghost and then decide iff'n you want to continue bein a couple and move in, 'cause you're a beautiful woman and could find another man easy, one without legs busted up like kindlin, burned on the outside like a overdone hamburger, dont have a job or much money, and looks to be talking to hisself and prob'ly should be locked up in the nuthouse over to Weston."

The disquisition had exhausted him. He took a gulp of wine, leaned back on the couch, and sighed. It would not have surprised him if Mary Robert had stood, reached for her coat, and walked out the door. Instead, she leaned over and topped off his glass, and while in that position turned her head and kissed him long and slowly.

She pulled back and looked at him. "Ever'body's crazy in some way or another. Your'n is jist a special kind of hit. I ain't scared of no ol' haint. They say a haint caint cross flowin water, so Jeeter ain't gonna git at us from acrost Scalded Crick." They laughed. "And besides," she added, "you axed me to decide, so I decided to decide this: I love you, and I'm a-comin hyur to live." She leaned over and kissed him again, and this time he kissed her back.

Skeeter said, "Anyhow, I think I done kilted him with my cane this afternoon. I was swingin it purty good tryin to knock a permanent hurt on his ugly ass when I toppled over. Mebbe the sumbitch is dead."

The voice whispered, "No, you dint kill me, fuck-head, but you'll kill us both one day iff'n you dont quit actin stupid. Git that woman out'n hyur, go pour that squirrel piss down the sink, and let's have us a cold beer."

"Her name ain't 'that woman.' Hit's Mary Robert, and she ain't goin nowheres."

Mary Robert grasped her third-party connection at once and said in Skeeter's ear, "Take that disquiet somewheres else, you mean ol' haint, or me and Skeeter liable to trade you in on a egg-suckin dog." Then she sat back and said, "Want me to give him a bloody nose, Skeet?"

◊ ◊ ◊

Then she confessed her secret to him. She once had uterine cancer, and a surgeon in the big hospital at Logan performed a hysterectomy. She could never have children, and she wondered if this might be a problem for Skeeter if they ever, you know, were to marry. He thought of his childhood and said that her condition was of no concern to him. She was relieved and said, "A-course hyur we be, livin in sin. People is talkin, a-course, but I never put much count in hit. I'll say hit loud and clear: I give nary a care what folks thinks 'cause they dont make sense anyhow. Like, if you give birth to a kid when you ain't married, you're a slut, but when you git married and have one folks thinks you're respectable."

Skeeter said, "Then hit dont matter iff'n we have sex and ain't married 'cause there caint be a kid any-ways. Reckon they won't be no bees swarmin at the Hatfield residence."

She laughed. "Oh you're a sly one, Skeeter Hatfield, though it matters to me 'cause I need someone who loves me permanent, and to me marriage is permanent, or ought to be."

A few days later Mary Robert walked in the door and got down on one knee. "Skeeter Hatfield, will you marry me? I gotta ax 'cause you prob'ly won't never figger out how, and also 'cause you caint complete the proposal motion. I'd have to yank you back up on your feet, and hit would spoil the romance of hit. So, answer me yes or no. A girl caint wait forever, which is a helluva lot more time than anybody has been give in this life by God or whoever." And that night she baked a huckleberry pie that was the best he had ever tasted.

◊ ◊ ◊

He was looking over the shelves at the company store when Sim Copley approached. He said in a confidential voice, "I seed you squirin Mary Robert, and rumor says you and her now livin together and gittin married. That girl, she ain't never gonna lose her vinegar."

"Hit ain't no secret, Sim."

"She's a fine lookin woman, Mary Robert, allus with a pencil stuck behind her ear when me and her do inventory. Keeps it right sharp too." He gave Skeeter a friendly elbow in the ribs. "She keepin your pencil sharp, Skeeter? I hyur they's some mileage on her tahrs, but a lotta tread still showin, iff'n you git my meanin." He squeezed a leer onto his face, then turned and sauntered down the aisle whistling.

◊ ◊ ◊

The preacher from Scalded Creek's little nondenominational church, a retired coal miner, married them in their living room in front of Mary Robert's parents and Sim Copley as witnesses. Odie Chafin was best man, and one of Mary Robert's friends from work was bridesmaid. Afterward, everyone drank champagne toasts to the newlyweds and a future life together and laughed good-naturedly about what kind of man marries a woman who once kicked his

ass. There was no honeymoon. That night Mary Robert joked that the *real* best man had been the ghost
of Jeeter Hatfield, and she whispered in Skeeter's ear,
"Listen up, ol' haint. Thanks fer not interruptin the
ceremony. I dint need the groom hollerin and swingin
his cane tryin to knock a hurt on your head."

◊ ◊ ◊

When bored with television they sometimes went to
Papaw's shed after supper, taking along popcorn and
a six-pack of beer or bottle of wine. In cold weather
they built a fire. They had installed a second chair.
Skeeter retold Papaw's stories about the Hatfields,
which had become fixed in memory after hearing
them repeated so often during his childhood. There
was the added drama of Jeeter's frequent interrup-
tions when he believed Skeeter had made a factual
mistake. When Skeeter paused, Mary Robert knew he
was listening. Skeeter had grown emboldened by her
presence, feeling as if they could gang up on Jeeter,
or at least conspire to keep him in line. On occasion,
he took Jeeter's advice and corrected himself; other
times he waved his left hand at the discarnate being
in back of him as if waving away a fly. Mary Robert
learned quickly to always sit on his right so as not to
be caught between them and receive an errant slap.

"I like you, Skeeter Hatfield. You ain't the dipshit I
allus thought you was."

"That's kindly of you Mary Robert Vance Hatfield,
long as you dont bloody my nose."

"Oh, I likely won't, and dont you pay no mind to

Jeeter," she said. "She leaned close to Skeeter's ear and said in a loud voice, "Now you listen up, Jeeter Hatfield. You're nothin but a mean ol' haint, and if you want to live hyur with me and Skeet you best straighten up or we'll put you outside amongst the other varmints." Then she sat back clapping her hands and laughing, and in an instant Skeeter was laughing with her.

He remembered as if it had happened yesterday and thought how strange that old memories often seem clearer than recent ones. He told Mary Robert the story of one of the few times he had straightened his shoulders and baited Jeeter, recalling the narrative and words as best he could.

They were there in Papaw's shed. "Papaw, I got a belly ache."

"Say agin?"

"I got a belly ache."

"Could be them soupbeans we et fer supper give hit to you. Need a trip to the garden-house, boy?"

"Not me. Hit's Jeeter needs to go." In his head Jeeter is saying, "Hit ain't me needs to shit, hit's you, liar! I'm a-gonna make you sorry."

"I dont care," he said aloud.

"Say agin? I caint hear you young-uns tonight. That cold wind's blowin hard. Reckon they's paper in the garden-house. Know that sayin 'tough as a cob?' Hit comes from times when they warn't paper and folks stored corn cobs in the garden-house. Hit could make fer a rough wipe when them cobs turned dry and hard. Then catalogues come along and my pa had a rule of a half of a page to a customer." He chuckled, then coughed. "We got store-bought'n toilet paper these days, and hit's why your buttholes is nice and soft and not all calloused up."

"Jeeter's really gotta go, Papaw." In his head, "Hit's *you*, shithead! You're gonna be sorry fer blamin hit on me."

"Well, ain't nobody stoppin him. Y'all go on. Git." And keep wearin them asaphidity bags your mama done hung round you necks to ward off colds." He flipped his hand in dismissal. "When y'all done your bidness go on up to bed. I figger on settin here and finishin my pipe, maybe take a drap or two out'n the jug. Close the door tight. G'night, young-uns."

"G'night, Papaw."

He ran for the back door as fast as he could, hearing Jeeter yell, "I'm right a-hint your sorry self. You caint run faster'n me!" But he got there first.

◊ ◊ ◊

The days passed, and she was in his life permanently: painting the dull walls, tossing out the smoke-stained curtains and replacing them with new ones she made, scrubbing the floors and suggesting new rugs. He capitulated, indifferent at first, then an enthusiastic ally.

"Honey, I'm home from work, and I got us a bottle of champagne."

"A bottle of what?" It was a joke they enjoyed pulling on each other, reprising the days when he was ignorant of wines.

"Bubbly wine rich folks drinks to celebrate."

"Cain't do us no good. We ain't rich. And what we

celebratin? We gittin married agin?"

"No, once is enough. How 'bout jist bein alive, bein together, havin somebody to love? We're celebratin we found one another and got a good life: a warm cabin, food, money comin in. My parents love you too, Skeet. Jist the other day I was joshin with Mama, and I said how you made a honest woman out'n me. And she laughed and said that I already was a honest woman up 'til I met with the likes of you." They laughed. "And Pa says he's real glad we got married, that you're a good man, and he's sorry fer your troubles." She rose and went to the kitchen, and he heard a pop.

Later in bed she said, "Champagne, the bubbles spillin out'n the bottle, each leetle bubble like one of your sperm cells. That's what hit feels like inside me, like this bottle overflowin and fillin me up. And the candle, hit's romantic, puts us in the mood. Does it put you in the mood, Skeet? It sure does me. I'm gonna put hickeys all over you." Her eyes seemed to reflect a peculiar glow in the candlelight, and he said he reckoned it did, alright, and that night they made love twice and once again the next morning.

◊ ◊ ◊

He sometimes thought about the fireteam and how his life might have turned out were it not for that mortar attack. Would he have gone to Michigan after mustering out and joined the assembly line making Chevys beside Weasel? Would he have tried ice fishing? It seemed incredible that guys could drive onto a frozen lake and set up camps to fish in midwinter. Weasel had described how they used gasoline-powered augers to drill holes through the ice then angle for perch and pike while sitting on stools in the bitter cold inside tents, bullshitting, smoking, and passing the bottle.

He remembered one night on bivouac, the world immersed in a tropospheric haze. You could hear the vegetation respiring, wallowing in its terrible wetness. He got up quietly to take a leak and saw Weasel standing guard, his outline barely visible. He was jerking off into the fecund tropical night, little huffs of lust merging with the trills of treefrogs and rhythmic breathing of the slumbering rainforest. Embarrassed, he crept away without being seen.

And Donut, knowing he was never going to be a farmer after his little sister's accident, was thinking of coming along too, but first he wanted Skeeter to visit him in Iowa and help fix his '48 Chevy pickup. Donut had described its condition and the model, but those details had long vanished from memory. He could stay at the farm until they got it running reliably, then the two of them would head to Michigan driving their respective trucks convoy style in case of a breakdown. That whole deal would have been a great adventure, he had told Mary Robert. Well, he would never know.

He missed those guys and Barnesie, but he missed Anax the most. Anax was the only one except Mary Robert and Odie who ever tried to help him and was sympathetic to his condition. It was Anax who had convinced him that the hallucinations might diminish with the proper state of mind. Anax had said that a strong sense of self was the key to ever controlling them and driving Jeeter into the background. Easier said than done, of course, but liking yourself and believing you are worthwhile might be possible with the help of a good friend and confidant. The first had been Anax himself, then Mary Robert, and after a couple of years he and Mary Robert had included Odie. He listened attentively as they explained the heautoscopic hallucinations and Jeeter's role. Then to their amazement he wept, the tears streaming in rivulets from his one eye. He said that no one had ever trusted him with such a secret or bared himself so openly. He was honored to have been told and honored to be a friend. He wiped his face and said, "Even though that sumbitch right thar shot out my eyeball!" He pointed at Skeeter, and they laughed.

Then Mary Robert added, "Leastways hit got you made 4F so's you dint come back from Vietnam lookin like roadkill!"

"Better not lay down in public, Skeeter," Odie said. "Lots of folks 'round here dont eat meat that ain't been shot or run over."

◊ ◊ ◊

Odie became a fuller part of their lives after that, and Mary Robert encouraged his friendship and presence. He seemed lonely, she said, and didn't have any family, and she knew that Skeeter needed companionship to relieve his boredom when she was working and Odie had a day off. In warm weather they fished or worked on their trucks. When the weather was bad they sat and talked, made minor repairs to the cabin, or went to Odie's and worked on his. Odie was often present for supper, contributing wine or beer, and either staying to watch television for an hour or two or accompanying them to Papaw's shed to build a fire and listen to stories of Hatfield history recounted by Skeeter. There was now a third chair, and sometimes when Skeeter hesitated and waved his left hand behind him it might be Odie who said, "Listen up, Jeeter. Hit's me, Odie, talkin at your earhole. We dont need the opinion of a shiftless haint. Jist let Skeeter tell the damn story his way." No matter the specific words, the situation was always good for a laugh. Imagine, they repeatedly told one another, three adults sitting before a fire admonishing a ghost.

And slowly Anax's advice took effect. The hallucinations diminished in both frequency and intensity, seeming to fade proportionately with age. As Skeeter expressed it once, "The older I git the less I give a shit." He had long since adopted Mary Robert's sunny outlook that life was good, and they had lots to be happy about.

Several times over the years the three had tried reading the entries in Anax's journal, barely starting before encountering a word or phrase that eluded them. The dictionary was of little help. Even later when the Internet came along and there were computers available for use in the public library at Man deciphering "the book" was finally declared hopeless, and during its last years in Scalded Creek it stayed in the dresser drawer.

◊ ◊ ◊

Odie died first. True to Anax's disdain of time and dates they did not record when the funeral was to be held and arrived late at the gravesite. The minister was just finishing his monologue, and the congregation was about to start reciting the Lord's Prayer. They stood behind the other mourners and wept silently. Mercifully, the cancer had taken Odie quickly, and he had borne the suffering stoically. They had been his caregivers, assisted by visiting nurses nearly to the end when hospice had taken over. Still, they were there, talking to him and holding his hand. Odie insisted on dying at home, and his wish was honored.

◊ ◊ ◊

They were well into their seventies when Mary Robert took the cancer. She had been experiencing back pain and a little urinary blood, so they scheduled a physical examination at the Logan Regional Medical Center, where the diagnosis was kidney cancer. She was put on a schedule of chemotherapy, and the side effects caused her to suffer more. She lost hair and weight, felt nauseous most of the time, and her food intake declined. The dark pouches under her eyes became permanent. It pained Skeeter to see her in this condition, knowing there was nothing he could do. Meanwhile, she seemed to worry more about him than herself, trying to smile and telling him not to worry. Chemotherapy came and went, and she rallied briefly, but it was a weak remission. She wore a hat to cover her baldness, and they went to a movie one evening. The excursion exhausted her. The next day she was too weak to get out of bed by herself. He took her back to the hospital, where she was advised to stay but refused, saying she would rather be home with her husband. She looked at Skeeter. Trying to grin, she said, "And our buddy, Jeeter." That would be enough, she insisted. She squeezed his hand, and they went home.

That night they went to bed early. She asked him to help her roll onto her left side so she could look at him before falling asleep. Mary Robert had always been a side-sleeper, normally on her right side facing away. It seemed a peculiar request, but he did as she asked. She said she was chilly, and would he please pull the bedclothes up to her neck.

He nodded off and awoke later in a silvery room magically awash in moonlight. Mary Robert felt cold. He looked closely at her face and noticed that her eyelids were partly open. He touched her neck and could not feel a pulse. He gently slid his arm under her torso and pulled her to him. Then came the sudden realization that their shared world was gone. They would never talk again and exchange special knowing looks, hold tightly to each other through times of laughter and pain. He squeezed her to him, stroking her hair and dissolving in wracking sobs. Her heat had passed into the cold of the room following the second law of thermodynamics. Her tissues and cells were already disintegrating into fundamental constituents. Entropy always wins.

◊ ◊ ◊

He did not weep at Mary Robert's burial, nor did his throat contract or emit even a hesitant sob. The anger and grief had been expended beforehand, and nothing more remained. All he could muster was a leaden sorrow that fell straight and true as a plumbline into eternity. Expressions of love in the presence of others do not require seepage of the lachrymal glands and the violent expunging of deoxygenated air.

The day was clear and cold with clouds stretched thin as pulled taffy. The few mourners huddled together like sheep, as if for warmth and safety. As he waited for the ceremony to end a mental image formed of Mary Robert standing in a mountain meadow. It was spring, and wind blew through her hair. She pushed it out of her face while turning toward him and smiling. How was it possible to conjure this scene but remain unable to describe it? How can words, even when turgid with context, nonetheless be empty, and why do their signifiers remain out of reach? For the same reason we can see the color blue but not describe its sensation. At such times, an inarticulate man's thoughts like those of a fine poet's remain unformulated, both entrapped in the knowledge that language is too superficial to express the depth of irrevocable sorrow.

His mind switched to Vietnam and a dim recollection of Anax's private lectures, to one in particular about how everything is in some sense a sign, that a sign stands in for something else and in doing so gives our lives metaphorical depth. Something perceived through the lens of something else is why nothing can ever be as it seems.

He was fading. There was not a place on his body that was pain-free. That nurse in San Diego of long ago had been right, that his feet would hurt for the rest of his life. So did his knees and back, his clavicle. Lifting either arm above the shoulder had become impossible. Yet he stood ramrod straight as if at parade rest, just as he had stood at Odie's funeral. It seemed an appropriate way of honoring them, while knowing that no one would notice. He was about to crumple when the service ended.

She was interred in the Hatfield section of the cemetery. His grave, when the time arrived, would be beside hers. Nearby were those of Mama and Pa and Mamaw and Papaw. He would lie between Mary Robert's grave and another's marked by a stone that stated:

JEETER HATFIELD
born December 31, 1941
died January 1, 1942

He had one chore left. "The book" was waiting on the passenger seat of the truck, the same truck he and Mary Robert had bought. After the funeral he would drive to the post office in Man and mail it to that library in Princeton. He would ask the clerk to put it in a sturdy box, the best available, and send it certified mail with a return receipt. That would be the last of his duties. What came after was irrelevant.

◊ ◊ ◊

His annual checkup that summer at the VA hospital had revealed what he already suspected: his weak heart had become weaker. The fluttering was

178

occurring more often, as were chest pains and the incidence of numbness down his left arm. The medication seemed ineffective. Caring for Mary Robert during the subsequent months had taken all his strength, and he found himself huffing and lightheaded while just fetching her a glass of water.

The night after the funeral and trip to the post office Jeeter came to him as he drifted into sleep. "Well, reckon hit's jist us agin, leetle brother. You glad?"

"I am and I ain't. I'm glad in a way not to be as lonely as I was after Mary Robert died, but sad 'cause hit's you hyur instead of her. You ain't been 'round much these last years, and hit's been a relief. But I'm grievous weary now and feelin a mite puny. Be gone out'n my earhole so's I kin sleep." He turned away, pulling the bedclothes over his head and feeling large and expansive, yet gathered within himself. For the first time he truly understood what Anax had meant by self-actualization.

But Jeeter would not leave it alone. "Skeeter, you dint listen close enough to what Anax was tellin us. Ever'body is in his own separate ego tunnel, and hyur you are, smack inside of your'n. Then what the hell am I doin inside hit with you? Shouldn't I ought'n to be in my own tunnel? See that light above? Iff'n hit ain't the light at the end of the tunnel then I dont know what is. Hit could only mean one thing: I'm your alter-ego, jist as Anax said, and not Jeeter's haint a-tall. I'm *you*, dumbass, and you been too fuckin stupid to figger hit out."

He turned and looked at the hallucination standing bedside. "On the night you was borned you shot

179

out'n the birthin chute hollerin holy blazes, sayin, 'Look at me! Look at me! Ain't I special?' Not right on my heels you dint, but prin near, and the same instant you drawed a first breath was the very same instant I let go my last. That's when I up and died, the same goddamn second you tuk to suckin air. Hit's like you done tuk *my* air from me and made it your'n. That's the minute when I give up the ghost, as the sayin goes. You kept livin and breathin while I got myself put away under the dirt. You was only a baby, but you knowed the timin of them events even without knowin 'em. Your ignorant baby mind suspected hit and kept on suspectin, is what I'm sayin, so when you was thinkin of me as a ghost all these years you was dead wrong, so to speak." He laughed sarcastically. "You reckoned I hated you all this time when hit was only you feelin guilty. I was dead, fer chrissakes!" He spread his arms for emphasis. "You shoulda got you a life somewheres along the road, as they say. Holy shit." His voice tailed off, and he shook his head in disbelief. "I dont know how to say hit, but hit's embarrassin to be related to such a dumb bastard as yourself, despite bein you too. Makes me wish I really was a haint."

His head was pulsing, the pain so fierce he was certain the skull bones were thinning and about to give way. His chest felt like an elephant was sitting on it. A sentence out of context formed in his mind, and he said, "One night the rain come in a sideways song and blowed a blast out of tune in our ears, 'til we turned up our collars and our backs."

Jeeter ignored him. "So, the deal is," he continued, "we're in superposition like that cat in the box that ain't neither alive nor dead 'til somebody lifts the lid and takes a look. Are we one, or two? Now, git out'n that bed, goddammit. We're a-gonna open the box. Iff'n you dont git up I'm a-gonna kick your ass!

"Like hell!" With effort he pushed off the bed-clothes and reached for his cane. It slipped from his fingers and clattered to the floor, and he fell on top of it. There he lay hurting all over and unable to move, the handle of the cane pressing into his temple. He opened the opposite eye to see Jeeter's hated grin inches away.

"Stand up, asshole. We're a-gonna race."

"Whar to?"

"To the light." Jeeter's face retreated until it became a silhouette surrounded by a blinding white glow. "That light. Don't you remember Anax tellin us about ego tunnels? Well, look up. That's the light at the end of our tunnel. Funny thing, though. As I said a-fore, ain't we supposed to have separate tunnels? What're we doin in the same one? I figgered hit out, but did you?"

He scrambled to his feet. The pain had disap-peared, and he felt young and supple. His visual per-spective zoomed out until Jeeter's entire outline was visible, still silhouetted against that piercing light that seemed to originate both above and behind his image.

"Ready, set, go!" Jeeter's silhouette turned in slow motion and started running away with exaggerated strides until disappearing into the light. He ran after it hearing echoes of Jeeter's laughter seemingly mixed with his own. They rose and fell in synchrony, quan-tum voices. The light dissipated, becoming white fire-works. He stopped to watch them unfold like alabaster flowers, languid and translucent. Jeeter's voice in the distance: "C'mon! You're late!"

He started running again, and when he glanced to the left there was Jeeter's hallucination loping beside him. They reached out and touched hands, and in an instant they merged into a common present like two photons in superposition. He felt the added mass gathered into him and a peaceful sensation of completeness. A moment later he broke through the moving wall of light, and on the other side was only a black emptiness, stark and soundless, stretching through infinity.